WINDY CITY DANGER

WINDY CITY DANGER 11

TYNDALE HOUSE PUBLISHERS, INC., CAROL STREAM, ILLINOIS

RED ROCK MYSTERIES

#1 BEST-SELLING AUTHORS

JERRY B. JENKINS · CHRIS FABRY

Visit Tyndale's exciting Web site for kids at www.tyndale.com/kids.

TYNDALE is a registered trademark of Tyndale House Publishers, Inc.

Tyndale Kids logo is a trademark of Tyndale House Publishers, Inc.

Windy City Danger

Copyright © 2006 by Jerry B. Jenkins. All rights reserved.

Cover and interior photographs copyright © 2004 by Brian MacDonald. All rights reserved.

Authors' photograph © 2004 by Brian MacDonald. All rights reserved.

Designed by Jacqueline L. Nuñez

Edited by Lorie Popp

Published in association with the literary agency of Alive Communications, Inc., 7680 Goddard Street, Suite 200, Colorado Springs, CO 80920.

Scripture quotations are taken from the *Holy Bible,* New Living Translation, copyright © 1996, 2004. Used by permission of Tyndale House Publishers, Inc., Carol Stream, Illinois 60188. All rights reserved.

For manufacturing information regarding this product, please call 1-800-323-9400.

Library of Congress Cataloging-in-Publication Data

Jenkins, Jerry B.
  Windy City danger / Jerry B. Jenkins, Chris Fabry.
    p. cm. — (Red Rock mysteries ; 11)
    Summary: While visiting Chicago, twins Ashley and Bryce catch up with old friends, visit the house where they grew up, see many reminders of their deceased father, and help search for their best friends' uncle, who disappeared days before his wedding.
    ISBN 978-1-4143-0150-1 (sc)
    [1. Missing persons—Fiction. 2. Christian life—Fiction. 3. Extortion—Fiction. 4. Twins—Fiction.
5. Chicago (Ill.)—Fiction. 6. Mystery and detective stories.] I. Fabry, Chris, date. II. Title.
  PZ7.J4138Win 2006
  [Fic]—dc22   2005028440

Printed in the United States of America

17   16   15   14   13   12   11   10
 9   8   7   6   5   4   3   2

To Meagan Rowell, dedicated reader.

"It is **BETTER** for a woman to marry a man who loves her than a man she loves."

Anonymous

"A **FRIEND** is one who knows us, but **LOVES** us anyway."

Father Jerome Cummings

"When a friend is in trouble, don't **ANNOY** him by asking if there is anything you can do. Think up something appropriate and **DO IT**."

E.W. Howe

PART 1

CHAPTER 1

MONDAY

❀ Ashley ❀

They say your life can change with a phone call. I don't know who "they" are, but they're right. It happened to me on a late-September night.

Bryce, my younger twin (by 57 seconds), and I were fighting over who got to sit at the head of the kitchen table to do homework. Dylan, our little brother, was jumping in the netted trampoline in our backyard, squealing into the wind. Leigh, our stepsister, was waiting for a call from her boyfriend. Sam, our stepdad, was late for dinner, and Mom was trying to throw something together at the stove.

Pretty much a normal evening until the phone rang.

"Timberline residence," I said.

"Ashley, you're not going to believe this! It's just the greatest!"

"I'm sorry. Who is this?"

It was Carolyn Hamilton, my best friend from Chicago. The one I had promised to write to every day and e-mail every hour when we moved to Colorado a few years ago. The one I hadn't talked with in ages.

We were going to prick our fingers and take a blood oath before I moved, but both of us got scared so we just spat in our hands and shook and promised we'd always be best friends. She's a year older than I am, but we were perfect for each other when I was in elementary school.

"What's going on?" I said. "Your brother getting married?" Tim is my age. He and Bryce used to play basketball and hang out together.

"You're not going to believe it," Carolyn said. I was getting tired of not believing something I didn't even know. "How would you like to come to Chicago and be in a commercial with me?"

She was right. I didn't believe it.

"My dad's advertising agency needs two kids for a commercial, and I remember how good you are at that kind of stuff."

Actually I don't like talking in front of people, but the last couple of years I've competed in forensics (speech) tournaments and feel comfortable as long as I know my lines.

"Want to do it?" Carolyn said. "My dad said they'd pay you."

"Sure. When?"

"This Thursday. You'd need to get here by Wednesday night."

I bit my lip as Mom stirred a pan on the stove. Looked like spaghetti. I had to convince her that this was a good-enough educational opportunity to miss school.

CHAPTER 2

◑ *Bryce* ◑

I'd been asking Mom for a year to let me go back to Ridgefield, our hometown in Illinois, and see my friends. No way was I going to let Ashley go back before me, so I was glad when Mom told her no, that she would miss too much school.

Ashley started crying. Leigh asked to use the phone, which was not good timing, and there were angry words. Ashley told Carolyn she'd call back and slammed down the phone.

I wished I'd made popcorn, because I like food with my entertainment.

When things get that hot, I usually try to find a way to leave, but

I kept my head down, listening to the pasta boil and Dylan squeal
outside.

"Mom, this would be perfect for me! I'd actually get to be in a
commercial! And Carolyn said I get paid!"

Mom seemed to be thinking about it as steam rose from the water. She'd known the Hamiltons a long time and had talked off and
on with Mrs. Hamilton over the past few years.

"I just don't think this is a good time," Mom said.

Ashley jumped on that. "So when *would* be a good time? I don't
think you'll ever let me go."

Mom held up a dripping wooden spoon, steam swirling from the
end. "Now don't go there. You know how much I let you do."

I went to our computer and pulled up the schedule for the Chicago Cubs. I'd been following them all season, but especially lately
as the season was near the end. The Web site said they were scheduled to return to Chicago Thursday for a make-up game with St.
Louis, their archrival.

"I'll go with her!" I yelled.

Mom and Ashley glanced at me like two boxers who'd just been
stopped by the referee. Neither seemed to like my offer.

"You know how I've been wanting to go back," I said. "I could
keep an eye on Lindsay Lohan here—"

"Hey, watch it!"

"Okay, I'll be your business manager and make sure they pay
you. Anyway, two for one seems like a pretty good deal. The house
will be really quiet."

Mom's face twisted into a little smile, but she regained her bull-
dog look in a flash. "Does this have anything to do with the Cubs?"

She sees everything, I thought.

CHAPTER 3

❀ Ashley ❀

Mom said she'd talk it over with Sam, and even that sliver of hope made me want to set the table. I didn't, of course, because it wasn't my night. But I did go to the front door and watch for Sam, knowing I'd have a better chance if I got to him first.

I thought of waiting for my real dad when I was younger. He drove a little silver car to the train station and rode to Chicago every day. I liked to stand at my bedroom window and then race downstairs and try to beat him to the driveway when his car came around the corner. He'd jump out of the car swinging his briefcase and wearing a big smile.

All that came to an end a few years ago when his plane crashed due to a terrorist attack. Sam's wife and young daughter were killed in the same crash, and Mom met Sam at one of the memorial services. The day we moved from Ridgefield to Colorado was the worst day of my life. The people moving into our house were already there as we pulled away. All my friends lined up, tears running down their cheeks. Part of me longed to go back just to see the house, but I'll admit the biggest part of me wanted to star in my first commercial.

I've told my journal this, but no one else knows that someday I want to act in a movie or be in a real stage play. As soon as Carolyn mentioned the commercial, I was sure some producer or actor would see it and call me to Hollywood. It's scary to share that kind of stuff with people, because they might laugh.

Truck brakes squealed as Sam pulled up and headed inside. He has a mustache that crinkles when he smiles. Tall, thin, sunburned, and handsome, with a growly voice, he reminds me of those Western movies where a guy tips back his hat to acknowledge "womenfolk." He carried a bag full of bread.

"You my welcoming party?" Sam said.

"You have to say yes," I said. "Carolyn called and it's the chance of a lifetime, but Mom is scared—"

"Hold on," Mom said behind me. She kissed Sam and pulled him into the kitchen. "No negotiating until *after* dinner."

CHAPTER 4

☺ *Bryce* ☺

I hate listening to silverware clink and Dylan slurp his spaghetti. (He calls it "pisgetti.") Nobody was talking—like the calm before a tornado. I felt lucky the spaghetti was really good—Mom had made fresh meatballs and lots of sauce, plus Sam brought two loaves of French bread that had just come out of the oven at Safeway.

I waited for the moment when I could spring the idea on him. We'd seen the Cubs play the Rockies at Coors Field, but going to Wrigley with the play-offs on the line was too good to pass up. I picked out some meatballs, made a sandwich, and waited.

Sam finally sat back with a smile and wiped his mouth with a napkin.

We all started talking at once (everyone but Dylan, whose face looked like a spaghetti graveyard), and Sam had to call for quiet. Mom was worried about Ashley going alone.

I jumped in. "I'll take care of her."

Ashley gave me a wicked stare.

Leigh said it wasn't fair that we got to miss that much school when Mom and Sam wouldn't even let her visit colleges until she was on break.

Ashley used the it'll-be-a-really-good-experience line, and I said it would be "nostalgic" going back and seeing the places our dad took us.

I regretted saying that when I realized how Sam might feel, but he didn't seem to mind. Things settled down, and we each got to say what we were thinking. Mom's voice cracked when she talked about how Ashley and I were growing up and all that mushy stuff.

Ashley asked if Sam could fly her, and Sam pursed his lips. "Probably be a lot cheaper to take a regular flight—that is, if you were to actually go."

"I have to!" Ashley said.

Sam held up a hand. "You two handle the dishes and clean up the Pisgetti Monster, and your mother and I will go talk about it."

Dylan raced over and buried his face in Sam's shirt. I think most guys would have held Dylan back, but Sam let him hug him until every red splotch was on his nice white shirt.

Dylan giggled and pointed as Sam walked outside with Mom. They took the path behind our house that leads to the red rock formation our town is named after. Mom had her arms crossed and shook her head as they started out. Then Sam took his hands out of his pockets and pulled her close as they disappeared behind the barn.

I've never seen Ashley clean the table so fast in my life. "What do you think my chances are?" she said.

"*Our* chances," I said. "I'm going with you."

"No way."

"Think about it. Mom won't let you go alone. Two heads are better than one and all that. You go to your commercial, and I'll go to the Cubs game."

"So this *is* about the Cubs."

I showed her the Web site.

"Better hurry," she said. "Looks like they're down to the bleacher seats."

I looked closer and almost said a bad word. *If I think a bad word, is it the same as saying it?*

It was too frustrating watching the ticket count go down every second, so I went outside to jump on the trampoline with Dylan. He still had spaghetti sauce on his clothes, and he looked like a bouncing meatball.

Ashley yelled that Sam and Mom were coming, and we rushed to the path. Mom's eyes were red, and I figured their conversation would show up in one of her books someday. She writes fiction under the name Virginia Caldwell.

"Have you decided?" Ashley said.

Mom nodded. "You can go—"

"Yeah!" Ashley screamed and did a victory dance.

Pippin and Frodo, our dogs, barked at the edge of the yard.

"I'm not finished," Mom said. "You can go if we can find a cheap flight *and* if your brother goes with you."

I did my own victory dance, which made Ashley laugh. Then I ordered a standing-room-only ticket for Thursday. By then even the bleacher seats were gone.

CHAPTER 5

❀ Ashley ❀

Mom called Mrs. Hamilton and talked for a long time. I heard laughing through her office door—a good sign—and Mom sighed a lot, as if talking with her brought back a lot of memories.

Bryce and I found the cheapest flight, which departed Wednesday at 6:00 a.m.

"I'll take you there and walk you to the gate," Sam said. "The Hamiltons will meet you at Midway Airport. Piece of cake."

I'd been so excited about the trip that I hadn't thought through all the stuff Bryce and I would need to do by ourselves. Going on a plane is one thing—going with just your twin felt like an adventure.

I couldn't wait, so I went to my room and laid out my clothes. Mom came and helped me sort through stuff.

"Remember when I used to sleep over at Carolyn's and take my horses?" I said.

"You had that little blue suitcase—"

"Strawberry Shortcake. I loved that."

I asked what Mrs. Hamilton had said, and Mom frowned. "They've been through some struggles, but I think they're okay." She ran her hand across the bedspread. "Sounds like you might not recognize Tim."

"I can't imagine he's changed *that* much. Probably still the same old Tim."

Mom said she'd buy Bryce and me some disposable cameras the next day so we could take a bunch of pictures. "You'll go by the old house, won't you?"

"Wouldn't miss it," I said.

As she was leaving, I said, "Mom, I know this is hard for you."

The light from my candle glistened in her eyes. I'll remember that look the rest of my life, because it said *I love you* without her even opening her mouth.

PART 2

CHAPTER 6

☺ *Bryce* ☺

It was one of those crisp, almost-October Colorado mornings when your breath swirls like smoke. Grass shivers.

The aspen trees near our house were turning from green to yellow. An aspen is a tall, skinny, white tree with leaves about the size of a 50-cent piece. They grow in groves, so you'll see a huge aspen and a lot of little aspens all around. A neighbor planted some a few years ago, and they've almost taken over his front yard.

Every year we drive west to a road filled with aspens, and it's like entering a golden forest. You'll see the green of the pine trees everywhere and then all of a sudden a shock of color that bursts like a sunbeam. Some groves you drive through make you feel like you've reached the yellow-leaf road.

Ashley and I loaded our stuff into Sam's truck and went back inside to say good-bye to Mom. She held us a long time—too long if you ask me—and kissed us. She tried to give us last-minute instructions, but her voice cracked.

Ashley said, "We know."

I guess when you think of all the bad things that happen to kids in their own backyards, it was pretty brave of Mom to let us fly to Chicago by ourselves. Plus, we did lose our dad in a plane crash, of course. She hugged us one more time, and Pippin and Frodo danced at our feet, wanting in on the action. Ashley and I knelt and gave them each a final pat on the head. Ashley let Frodo lick her face, but I thought it was disgusting.

It was too dark to see any of the aspens as we drove north on I-25. Too dark to see much of anything except car dealerships and stores lit with overhead lights. Sam put the radio on to check for traffic and looked at his watch every few minutes. Ashley put her head back and went to sleep, but there was no way I could do that. I guess that's one of the differences between us—she can sleep on airplanes, on trains, and in cars. I think she could even sleep on a snowmobile if someone else was driving. I stay awake until the bitter end.

Sam took the tollway, and a little more than an hour after we left we were pulling into the big parking garage at DIA—Denver International Airport.

We stood in line while Sam checked our bags and got a temporary ticket so he could take us to our gate. Then we went down the escalator and stood in another line at the security checkpoint. Since we were only 13 and didn't have driver's licenses, we brought our birth

certificates. We put our jackets and shoes through the X-ray ma-
chines, then walked through the metal detector.

I made the thing go off like a fire alarm before I remembered my
cell phone. I had to show the guard that the phone worked. Then he
made me hold my arms out and waved a wand around me. I felt like
a criminal. I wanted to say something funny, but airport-security
people are touchy—even about jokes. You can get into a lot of trouble. And after what happened to my real dad, I didn't want to tease
people who were here to keep us safe.

Sam kept looking at his watch, and they finally let me put my
shoes back on. We went down the escalator to the train, and it took
another few minutes to reach Concourse A.

My stomach growled as we passed McDonald's. I wanted a sausage biscuit so bad I could taste it, but Sam told us to keep going. The
plane was already boarding when we got to the gate.

CHAPTER 7

❀ Ashley ❀

"Have a good time," Sam growled, handing us each a white paper bag. He wasn't emotional, but I couldn't help thinking that the last time his loved ones had flown without him, he never saw them again.

On the plane we stuffed our things in the overhead bin, and I took the window seat. Bryce had dibs on it for the trip back.

We sat through the instructions on how to fasten your seat belt, where the emergency exits were, and what to do "in the unlikely event of a water landing." Unlikely was right. There wasn't much chance of that between Colorado and Illinois, but I guess you have to cover all the bases.

I opened my white bag and found a sausage biscuit, hash browns, and a 50-dollar bill with a sticky note attached. *Have fun with this,* Sam had written.

It almost made me cry, but I was too hungry.

"Did you get a hundred too?" Bryce said.

I gaped at him, and he laughed, holding up his 50.

I ate as we pulled back from the ramp. The pilot's voice came over the intercom and welcomed us, told us how high we'd fly, our scheduled landing time, the temperature in Chicago (already 15 degrees warmer), and the time there. We set our watches an hour ahead for Central time.

I haven't flown a lot, but every time we lift off the ground, I think of the statistic that most airplane crashes happen at takeoff or landing. I closed my eyes. *Father, keep us safe, but if it's my time, I'm ready.*

I wasn't sure I was really ready, but when you're a Christian, you don't have to be afraid of death.

I was glad when we shot into the air.

CHAPTER 8

ⓤ *Bryce* ⓤ

The ground looked like patches of a quilt. A lot were brown, but the farther east we traveled, the more colorful things got. Huge sections of yellow wheat gave way to green corn. The closer we got to Illinois, the more colorful the trees looked. It reminded me of the pile of leaves in our Ridgefield backyard and the huge oak tree there. I couldn't wait to see the old neighborhood.

Most of the other passengers looked like businesspeople—nicely dressed and using laptop computers. There was a family with two little kids, and the boy reminded me of Dylan. I'd been gone only a few hours, and already I missed the little guy.

Ashley had her head against the window, which made me wonder why anyone would sleep in a window seat. I read a magazine and tried a crossword puzzle. I'm not very good at that kind of thing, but it passed the time. The flight attendant brought around bagels, but I was stuffed. I drank Dr Pepper, and that woke me up.

We finally descended, and I picked out the skyline of Chicago, shrouded in smog. We circled an industrial section with lots of train tracks and smokestacks. As we dipped above homes, I could pick out every trampoline and pool behind each house.

When we landed and taxied to the terminal, the pilot asked everyone to stay seated, but as soon as the plane stopped, everyone got up and opened the overhead bins.

The first thing I noticed in the terminal was the heat and humidity. In Colorado, the air feels light and cool most of the year. Here the air is heavy and damp, like you're walking into a sauna. It wasn't too hot, but I was glad we weren't here in July when it's really bad.

Mrs. Hamilton had said she would meet us in baggage claim, so we checked the monitors for which carousel would have our luggage, then followed the crowd. We passed all kinds of restaurants and shops, most selling Chicago Cubs hats, shirts, mugs, and pennants. We also saw Bears and White Sox stuff, but most places put the Cubs front and center.

We made it to the carousel but didn't see Mrs. Hamilton. I found my duffel bag, and Ashley got her rolling suitcase.

"Think we should call her?" Ashley said. "Maybe we're supposed to meet her somewhere else."

My cell phone rang. I answered and put it on speaker mode so Ashley could hear.

"There's an emergency here," Mrs. Hamilton said. "I can't come to the airport so we're sending a limo. Stay right where you are."

CHAPTER 9

❈ Ashley ❈

"No, don't do that, Mrs. Hamilton," Bryce said. "I have another idea."

A homeless guy looked like he was listening. Other people ignored us.

"Look," Bryce said, "Ashley and I used to go downtown on the train with our dad. We'll just hop the Orange Line, go downtown, and transfer. No problem."

Bryce was a lot more convincing than I would have been. I would've taken a cab or waited for the limo, but his boldness rubbed off on me. I did want to go downtown.

"I'm sure Mom wouldn't have a problem with it," Bryce said, "and it sounds like it would help you. I'll call when we're coming your way, and someone can pick us up at the station."

The homeless guy edged closer. It smelled like he hadn't had a bath in a decade, and his eyes were red and hollow looking. "Need to know where the train is?" he said.

I moved away. "I don't have any money. . . ."

Bryce closed his phone and said, "Yeah, which way to the Orange Line?"

The man laughed, and that started him coughing. When his lungs cleared he said, "Just go through there, up to the second floor, and across the walkway. You can buy your token there . . . with the money you don't have."

"I'm sorry—"

He shook his head and laughed and coughed again. "You kids get outta here. You're taking up space in my airport."

CHAPTER 10

☺ *Bryce* ☺

I knew the trip would be an adventure, but I'd had no idea we'd get to go to my favorite restaurant on the planet—Carson's. I could almost taste their ribs and coleslaw as we reached the ticket kiosk. The problem was, neither Ashley nor I knew how to work it. The directions were confusing, and farther up people crowded through turnstiles.

I was about to put a couple of dollars in when Ashley got a CTA (Chicago Transit Authority) attendant's attention. I told him we wanted to stop at Carson's restaurant downtown before heading to Ridgefield.

"Ah, great choice." He put our money in and told us which trains to take and when to use the tickets.

Ashley and I followed the crowd down an escalator, lugging our stuff. Ashley had it best because her suitcase has wheels.

We found a couple of seats, and I studied a chart on the wall that showed all the stops. To say we were the youngest people on the train is an understatement, and we got some interesting looks. Like on the plane, some people were dressed nicely, obviously heading for work, and others looked like they'd been jogging or had been sleeping on the train.

I didn't feel scared, but I was really glad Ashley was here. I checked and rechecked that my wallet was in my front pocket. If I lost it, I was in big trouble. I figured the $50 would cover the lunch easily.

"So what do you think the Hamiltons' emergency was?" Ashley said.

"No idea."

"Must be pretty bad."

"Either that or they forgot."

"They didn't forget. You don't think Carolyn or Tim is hurt, do you?"

I shrugged.

Later we got off at the right stop, found the platform for the next train, and made it to Clark Street. We figured out which way Lake Michigan was, noticed an old McDonald's our dad used to take us to, then went west until we reached Carson's. It had the yellow sign out front like I remembered, the same photos of sports stars and politicians on the walls, and the same dark interior.

The guy at the front raised his eyebrows and stared at our luggage. "Just the two of you?"

"Yeah," I said.

"Smoking or non?" he said, grinning. Guess it was obvious we were a little young for that.

"Big-time non," Ashley said.

The first taste of coleslaw was like a mouthful of the past. I imagined my dad in the seat across from us, smiling, enjoying his barbecue-pork sandwich. I think food is for more than just keeping our bodies going. Jesus used food to teach, held the Last Supper, and ate with his disciples after he resurrected. I think I've laughed the hardest and had some of the best times at cookouts and restaurants.

The coleslaw was so good that I ordered another, and the waitress didn't even charge me. "It's on me, kid," she said.

CHAPTER 11

❃ Ashley ❃

My arm was tired from pulling the heavy suitcase, and I wished I'd packed light. We headed back to the train but got turned around. Bryce pointed at the Sears Tower and said it was just like the mountains in Colorado—you could always tell which direction to go if you could see it.

My excitement about being in Chicago was overshadowed by what had kept the Hamiltons from picking us up. I hoped Mom didn't know we were traipsing around the city alone. When we finally found the right train, I asked to use Bryce's phone.

"I pay by the minute," he said.

The train clattered along as I dialed Mrs. Hamilton's cell phone. She answered with a shaky voice, and I told her we were on our way.

"Ashley, I feel awful about not being there to pick you up. You must think we're terrible."

There were strange noises in the background, like someone on a loudspeaker.

"Well, we had a nice lunch and got to walk around downtown. Is Carolyn with you?"

"She's still at school. She'll be out the rest of the week, so we didn't want her missing more days."

"So she's not in trouble?" I said. "Is it Tim?"

"No, thank goodness. It's actually . . . can you hold a minute?"

Bryce snapped his fingers and pointed at his watch.

"Ashley," Mrs. Hamilton said, "the police are calling. I'll talk to you later."

CHAPTER 12

☺ *Bryce* ☺

I remembered riding this same train with our dad.
I could almost point to the seats we sat in. The billboards outside had changed, but the houses seemed the same.

Our lives had changed a lot since moving to Colorado. Our family was different—with two new members who weren't Christians. We'd settled into the routine of living in a small rural town, but coming back here made me miss Chicago.

At the Ridgefield station we lugged our stuff onto the platform, and I found a bathroom while Ashley called the Hamiltons again.

When I came back, Ashley's face was white. "Mom called."

"You didn't tell her . . ."

"She'd called Mrs. Hamilton. She wanted to know why we didn't tell her what was going on."

"Maybe we should have. Was she mad?"

"Well, she wasn't exactly having a party. She was glad to know we were okay. Mrs. Hamilton is on her way."

I sat by Ashley, and we watched people come and go. At the little pond near the station a bunch of geese landed in perfect formation.

"Can you believe we're actually back?" I said.

"Feels like we never left."

When Mrs. Hamilton finally arrived, she drove us through the old neighborhood, and I was amazed at how pretty the trees looked. The leaves had begun to change. Another couple of weeks and these streets would look like rainbow forests.

We passed our old elementary school and the path we had walked every day. Ashley and I just stared, pointing out where Mr. Mickey had been our crossing guard.

"There it is," Ashley whispered.

We passed our house, and Mrs. Hamilton could tell we wanted to get out. "We'll have to come back later," she said.

Our house looked smaller, and I couldn't believe we actually used to sled down the little hill in front. The driveway and bushes were small, and all the houses seemed a lot closer together. I guess I had become used to Colorado, where the houses are football fields apart.

We turned down the Hamiltons' street and found kids walking home from the high school and middle school bus stops. Carolyn saw the car, and her face lit up like a fireworks display.

I didn't see Tim. There was a guy walking close to Carolyn. If that was her boyfriend, I figured she was in big trouble.

CHAPTER 13

❀ Ashley ❀

I jumped out and hugged Carolyn. The guy in a dark leather jacket behind her looked like someone out of a horror movie. Black hair down to his shoulders. A ring through his nose. A chain hung from one of his pockets and caused his pants to hang way past his underwear line. He smirked at me.

"I'm so glad you came!" Carolyn said. "I've got so much to tell you."

"Aren't you going to say hi?" Leather Jacket said.

"Do I know you?"

Carolyn laughed. "You don't recognize Tim?"

I tried to shut my mouth.

Bryce grabbed his hand in their old handshake, as if he had known it was Tim all along. "Looking good," Bryce said, then turned to me with a what-happened-here? look.

As soon as we got inside, Mrs. Hamilton peppered us with questions about Dylan, Mom, and Colorado. Tim didn't last long and went upstairs.

When I could get a word in, I said, "So what's going on around here that involves the police?"

Mrs. Hamilton glanced at Carolyn, then back at me. Finally she said, "My brother-in-law, Larry, is getting married Saturday. We figured you and your brother could take that time to walk through the neighborhood or see other friends."

"That's fine," I said, "but is there something wrong?"

She nodded. "His fiancée, Peggy, called this morning. Larry's missing."

"How long?" Bryce said.

"No one at work has seen him since Monday. I went over to his house. We have a key just in case he gets locked out or something. Everything looks normal. He's just vanished."

"What about his car?" I said.

She hesitated, then said, "Gone."

"What kind of work does he do?" Bryce said.

"He owns an Internet company," Carolyn said. "He hired me this past summer to type and take phone calls. The office is about five minutes from here."

"So you called the police?" I said.

Mrs. Hamilton nodded. "They don't do much in the first 24 hours. I just hope he turns up in time for the wedding."

CHAPTER 14

☺ *Bryce* ☺

A thousand thoughts went through my mind. It was another mystery and right in our old hometown. Why would a guy about to get married disappear?

Maybe he'd gotten cold feet and was a runaway groom. Mrs. Hamilton showed us a picture of Larry and Peggy together at some tennis tournament. Peggy was beautiful—long, dark hair, a smile that would melt butter, and a sweetness you could see even in pictures. She looked like Lynette Jarvis from my class in Colorado, though Lynette's nature was more like that of a velociraptor.

Maybe somebody kidnapped him and wanted a ransom. But why would they hold him hostage?

"Does Larry have a lot of money?" I said.

"He does well, and there's talk that a bigger company might buy his company out, but he's not rich," Mrs. Hamilton said.

"How did they meet?" Ashley said, looking at the picture. That was something I wouldn't have thought to ask.

"In church. Larry's a little older than Peggy and is a deacon there. She had asked for someone from the church to check her car, and Larry got the assignment."

"Love at first tune-up?" I said.

Mrs. Hamilton smiled. "It's been eight months since their first date. Not long after that, Larry hired her to work at his office." She ran a hand through her hair. "I just can't imagine . . ."

The phone rang and Mrs. Hamilton stood. As she walked into the kitchen, Carolyn helped bring our bags upstairs. Pictures of the family covered the wall: Carolyn's and Tim's silhouettes as grade schoolers, the family at some campground, Christmas when they were little, stuff like that. I remembered this staircase a lot wider and taller. In fact, the whole house seemed smaller.

I put my suitcase outside Tim's door. Music blared from inside, and it sounded like Tim's tastes had changed. We used to listen to music as we played basketball outside. He was into Christian bands back then, but either this was a Christian band I'd never heard, or it was one of those head-banging groups they play on the Mickey and Maury show back home. I don't listen to Mickey and Maury, but I know what they play.

"I'd understand if you don't want to stay in there," Carolyn said. "You can sleep on the pullout couch in the rec room if you want."

"Maybe I will," I said, moving into Carolyn's room. "What happened to him?"

Carolyn shrugged.

The doorbell rang and Ashley looked out the window. "It's the police."

CHAPTER 15

❊ Ashley ❊

We listened from the top of the stairs as the police told Mrs. Hamilton they would start talking with people in Larry's office if he was still unaccounted for after 24 hours.

Mrs. Hamilton asked questions the police couldn't answer.

Then the officer asked if there was anyone who might know more about Larry, a close friend he might have confided in.

"He's friends with people at church. Our pastor. His best friend is Dave over at the office, though. I'm sure if anyone knew anything—"

"As far as we're concerned, nothing is wrong yet. He'll probably show up in a couple of hours, and everyone will have a big laugh over this."

Mrs. Hamilton didn't laugh.

As the officer left, Bryce grabbed his stuff and went downstairs.

Carolyn and I moved back to her room. "You think your dad will go ahead with the commercial?"

"Dad?" Carolyn said, smirking. "He'd work the day of his own funeral. He'll say that Larry's always been a little fickle and there's nothing we can do, so we ought to go ahead with our plans."

"You have the script?"

She pursed her lips. "You're girl number one."

CHAPTER 16

☾ *Bryce* ☾

When I finally checked in with Mom by phone, I almost wished I hadn't.

"I'm glad you got to eat at Carson's," she said. "And I'm glad you made it okay and you're safe, but you don't have any idea what can happen to two kids walking around Chicago!"

I apologized and tried to steer the conversation to the emergency, but Mrs. Hamilton had already filled Mom in.

"I'm surprised she didn't mention the wedding to me before we sent you out there," Mom said.

"Sounds like there might not be one," I said.

Mom took a breath, and I knew what was coming. "Sam and I don't think you should go to the Cubs game alone."

"Mom, I only have one ticket. And with all that's going on here, do you think I'll find anybody to go with me?"

"We don't like it, Bryce. It's too dangerous."

The Mom-I'm-not-a-little-kid line didn't work, so I tried the Wrigley-Field-and-memories-of-Dad approach. That slowed her a little.

"I'll call you at every stop," I said. "I'll call you between pitches. I'll call the police if I see anyone remotely suspicious."

I imagined her smiling.

"Please, Mom. It's the Cubs. They might make the play-offs. It's the chance of a lifetime."

CHAPTER 17

❦ Ashley ❦

If this was the path to Hollywood, I wasn't sure I wanted to be on it. The script for the furniture store was dopey, and though Carolyn and I tried hard to make it better, I felt like we were going to bomb.

"Don't worry," Carolyn said. "Dad can make it work during production."

Mr. Hamilton was over six feet tall with a round face, a pencil-thin mustache, and a smarmy smile. I remembered not wanting to come to Carolyn's house sometimes because he was kind of mean, but the more I got to know him, the more I realized it was just the way he was. Intense. Focused.

At dinner that night he told his wife, "Larry's a little flighty. There's nothing we can do other than go ahead with the plan."

Mrs. Hamilton put down her fork. "Go ahead with the wedding even though half the couple is missing?"

Her husband dabbed at his mouth. "He's probably on some personal retreat or just getting his head together," he said, popping a whole egg roll into his mouth. "This is a big step for him. He's been single a long time."

"If that's all it was, he'd have told someone," Carolyn said.

Mrs. Hamilton went upstairs to get Tim, but I could tell it was just an excuse to leave the room and let off some steam. I've seen that walk before.

"So, how do you like Colorado?" Mr. Hamilton said. I doubted he even remembered our names.

We told him about our ATVs, our trips to the mountains, skiing, hiking, fishing, biking, and all the animals that come around our house. He seemed interested—for about 15 seconds. Then he went into some other world and switched the subject to our commercial shoot the next day.

"We'll need to leave no later than seven, so be up and ready. Don't worry about makeup—we'll do that when we get there."

Mrs. Hamilton returned without Tim and winced at her husband. I guessed this happened a lot. Sam and Mom have had problems with Leigh, but Tim's situation seemed worse.

"What are you up to tomorrow?" Mr. Hamilton asked Bryce.

Bryce told him about the Cubs game, and the man's eyes lit up. "If I didn't have this shoot, I'd be right with you."

When dinner was over Mr. Hamilton told his wife, "I'm going to have a look at Larry's house."

"Can we go?" I said.

He looked at me like I'd suggested he drink a kung-pao milk shake.

"Bryce and Ashley are really good at figuring out stuff," Carolyn said. "Ashley's told me they've solved mysteries in Colorado."

Mr. Hamilton shrugged. "Why not?"

CHAPTER 18

☺ *Bryce* ☺

I guess most kids wouldn't care about an empty house, but I was excited. Looking for clues is my idea of fun. And it's rewarding. I can see myself growing up to become a detective or a private investigator or a crime-scene person catching bad guys and putting them away. I think making the world a safer place would be a pretty good job.

If I could be a major league baseball player, that wouldn't be too bad either. Or an announcer for the games. Or maybe a baseball detective. Hmm.

My great powers of observation told me Larry was a Cubs fan.

The blue-and-white mailbox with the *C* on it was my first clue. The side even had a little baseball flag that popped up. Mr. Hamilton grabbed the envelopes and catalogs from it.

A wooden porch was decorated with nice plants in large planters, and the wood looked new, like it had been recently stained. Two rocking chairs in the corner were in perfect condition.

The house smelled stale. In the kitchen trash I found two Domino's Pizza boxes and some half-eaten slices. Dishes were piled in the sink, and dirty paper plates lay on the counter. Flies buzzed about. We don't have that many in Colorado—I guess they like living closer to sea level.

"Try not to touch anything," Mr. Hamilton said. "The police said they might want to search the place once Larry's been missing 24 hours."

Ashley and Carolyn picked through the mail while I went through each room. Except for the kitchen, it was obvious Larry was a neat person who liked things in their places. Beds were made. Towels hung straight on their racks. Carpets were vacuumed. In fact, you could still see the lines the sweeper had made in one room.

At the end of the second-floor hall I carefully turned a doorknob and gasped at Cubs posters, Cubs jerseys, Cubs bats in glass cases, an Ernie Banks autographed glove, and a lot more. I had a lot in common with Larry.

On one wall were pictures of Larry with numerous Cubs players through the years—Ryne Sandberg, Andre Dawson, Mark Grace, Kerry Wood, and others. Another shot showed a little boy with his front teeth missing standing with an older man in front of Wrigley Field. The caption read "Larry and Dad."

Another picture showed Larry with a bunch of people in the

stands, holding up a sign for his company. It made sense that they'd have an outing at his favorite place.

What didn't make sense was why Larry would miss the most important game of the season—not to mention his own wedding. Unless he was hurt or worse.

"Larry was hooked the first time he walked into Wrigley," Mr. Hamilton said behind me. He gazed at the walls like he was viewing a museum of his brother's life. "Baseball was all he cared about when he was a kid."

"You too?" I said.

"I was a White Sox fan. Still am. So's my wife. Cubs are just losers in our book." He picked up a laminated Sammy Sosa card. "Sosa played for the White Sox before he went to the Cubs, you know that?"

I nodded. "Did Larry go to a lot of games?"

"He has season tickets." Mr. Hamilton opened a drawer and rummaged until he found a stub. "This is his seat behind home plate."

I asked where the tickets for the rest of the year were.

He shrugged. "Maybe he has them with him. He's trying to get tickets for the postseason."

When Mr. Hamilton wandered out, I jotted the row and seat number on a scrap of paper and stuck it in my pocket. I went back downstairs and glanced out the window.

A shadowy figure looked back.

CHAPTER 19

❀ Ashley ❀

Carolyn followed me around like I was some kind of sleuthing expert. I'm not, but I'm getting better. Problem was, nothing looked out of the ordinary in Larry's house. At least for a bachelor.

I checked the caller ID on his phone for any suspicious numbers. "One comes up pretty often," I said.

"That's Peggy's cell phone," Carolyn said.

I could only imagine how frantic his fiancée must have been.

Bryce raced out of a back room and headed for the front door. "Somebody's out there!"

We followed him down the steps and around the corner. He burst through some bushes and looked both ways.

"Maybe it was a neighbor," Carolyn said.

Bryce ran down the street while Carolyn and I went into the yard. A high wooden fence ran the length of the back. There was no place to hide, except a small shed, and that was locked. Mr. Hamilton said that was where Larry kept his lawn mower and tools.

I could tell Mr. Hamilton thought Bryce was seeing things, but I know my brother well enough to know he doesn't make stuff up.

It was dark by the time we got back to Carolyn's house, and a car stood in the driveway.

A pretty woman with dark hair sat in the living room, dabbing at her eyes. She wore a Cubs necklace and matching earrings.

We introduced ourselves to Peggy and told her we were sorry about Larry.

Larry's fiancée seemed to be trying to put on a happy face. When Mrs. Hamilton and Carolyn went into the kitchen to get some tea, Bryce and I had a chance to talk with Peggy.

"Was Larry acting any different the past few weeks?" I said.

Peggy shook her head. "He worked his normal schedule, we watched the Cubs over the weekend, and we made plans for our honeymoon."

"Where are you going?" Bryce said.

"Cooperstown, New York, the National Baseball Hall of Fame. There's also a bed-and-breakfast in Maine where we're spending a week." Her chin quivered. "I was looking forward to that so much."

"Did he get any weird phone calls?" I said.

Peggy pressed her lips together and appeared to be thinking. "There was one time—it was during Sunday's game against Washington. He answered and said to hang on. Then he went into the other room. He seemed tense after that. He said it was just business."

CHAPTER 20

◉ *Bryce* ◉

Tim didn't seem to want Ashley and me in his house, let alone to talk to me after I'd first seen him. I figured he wouldn't hear me over his booming music, but I knocked anyway, and he finally opened the door. He stared at me.

"Mind if I come in?"

He turned and sat on his bed. "Close the door behind you."

I sat on a lawn chair as far from his speakers as I could. His uncle Larry's special room had been blue and white for the Cubs. Tim's was black and red for death and blood. Posters of bands that looked more like zombies than musicians covered his walls. One wall looked like an elephant had put black and purple paint in its snout and sprayed.

"Interesting room," I said.

He laid back, hands behind his head.

"So, where'd you get the nose ring?"

"Same place I got this." He pulled up his sleeve and showed me a tattoo.

"I thought you couldn't get one until you were 18."

"It's 21 here, but you can get anything if you know where to go."

"What did your parents say?"

"Who cares?"

I couldn't believe it. Tim had always been such a good guy. He loved doing stuff with his dad—at least when his dad was around. I sighed. "What do you think happened to your uncle?"

He shrugged. "Ask his church friends. He's tight with those people."

I nodded and sat thinking. Then I said, "Tim, I don't know what's happened to you since I left, but if you want to talk about it . . ."

He looked at me like I was a dead skunk. "What are you talking about?"

"The kid I used to play basketball with, the one I went fishing with, who'd come over to our house and camp out in the backyard—what happened to him?"

"I grew up." He shook his head. "You're just like them. You want me to be a little kid."

"We've all grown up, Tim. But you must have some new friends."

"So? Don't you?"

"I moved to Colorado. I had to make new friends."

"Fine, Bryce, why don't you go back?"

He cranked the music louder, but I heard a knock over the din and opened the door. It was Mrs. Hamilton telling me my mom was on the phone. "Coming," I said.

I turned back to Tim. "I was hoping to go to school with you Friday and see some friends."

"Whatever."

PART 3

CHAPTER 21

THURSDAY

❀ Ashley ❀

Carolyn and I stayed up past midnight talking about boys and memorizing the script. With all the traveling, I was asleep as soon as my head hit the pillow.

Carolyn woke me at 6:00, and Mrs. Hamilton had muffins for us. I couldn't eat even half of one. My stomach was flipping like an Olympic gymnast.

Mr. Hamilton was all business, his cell phone ringing to the tune of "Money," an old song by Pink Floyd. He went on with his life like nothing was wrong, but it was obvious from his wife's face—not to mention two calls from Peggy already—that Larry was still missing.

We drove past our old elementary school, and I wanted to cry. So much had happened to us at that school. Concerts, competitions, tests, reports. I remembered how excited I was to get into Mr. Ramsey's "upstairs" third-grade class and the day I was given the safety patrol of the year award.

A kindergarten class romped on the playground, and I told Carolyn, "I can't believe we were ever that little."

"*You* were that little. I was a lot more mature. Remember the crush you had in first grade? Freddie McCarty."

"Freddie!" I squealed. "I'd forgotten all about him and his little glasses."

"Freddie's wearing contacts now. Saw him at a football game last week. He's really cute."

We talked about our most embarrassing moments—the time Carolyn's pants split in gym class, when I tossed my cookies in the lunchroom during pigs-in-a-blanket day, and the lines we both forgot during performances of songs and skits. Remembering all that helped me forget, at least for a few minutes, how nervous I was.

The parking lot at the furniture store was empty, except for a blue van and another car.

The store owner—a large man with a huge nose—held the door for a muscular guy lugging camera equipment. A short man with hair that flipped up over his head and stood on end like a lion's mane paced and talked into a cell phone.

"That's Granger, the director," Mr. Hamilton said. "He'll tell you exactly what he wants. And the camera guy is Dustin. Follow their lead and you'll do fine."

I prayed he was right.

CHAPTER 22

☺ *Bryce* ☺

I slept until 8:30 and woke with a stiff neck and a sore back, probably from the long day carrying luggage and the long night on a couch as soft as a marshmallow.

Mrs. Hamilton was on the phone a lot during breakfast, answering calls about Larry from people at their church.

When she hung up, I said, "Is there still a chance the wedding will happen Saturday?" It was a dumb question, because without Larry there wasn't a wedding, but I had to say something.

"We have to cancel the restaurant and the cake and . . ." She sat and put a hand to her head. "I have to go to Larry's office and talk with people there."

"Mind if I go along?"

CHAPTER 23

✖ Ashley ✖

The production was set up in the corner of the warehouse behind the main showroom. It took forever for Dustin to position the lights. He moved them to one side, then the other, then moved them back, then forward.

Carolyn and I put on our own makeup, per Granger's direction—this was a pretty low-budget affair. The script called for two typical teenagers standing in front of a living-room suite. I would sit in a huge recliner and say my line, and then we'd show off a bedroom.

I knew it might take a long time because I'd been to the filming of a movie in Chicago once. The scene was just a guy walking to his car

64 JENKINS • FABRY

with a cell phone to his ear and driving away. It took almost six hours to shoot, and the crew said it went well.

After Carolyn and I ran through our scenes, Granger spoke with Dustin, then gestured wildly as he talked with Mr. Hamilton.

"Maybe he doesn't like us," Carolyn said.

My stomach was growling like a caged leopard.

Mr. Hamilton came over. "You guys are doing great. Granger likes you both. He wants you to loosen up a little, but he has a backup script he thinks will be even more, ah . . . effective."

"New lines?" I said.

"Won't be hard. I promise. We just have to wait for the wardrobe change."

CHAPTER 24

☺ *Bryce* ☺

On the way to Larry's office, Mrs. Hamilton told me he had started his own Internet business, something to do with real estate and selling houses. He started in Ridgefield and expanded to other towns, then to Chicago, and from there it took off. Now they were in 38 states, including Hawaii. Mrs. Hamilton said she wouldn't be surprised if some big company bought them out.

"How much is the company worth?" I said.

"Millions," she said.

Maybe that was someone's motive, but what had they done with Larry?

The business was located in a typical brick-and-glass building, except at the top a single office stuck up like the gun turret of a tank, with windows on all four sides.

We rode the elevator to the fourth floor, where Larry's partner and best friend, Dave Jokic, worked in the top office. We went up a winding staircase, and Dave hugged Mrs. Hamilton. He was a round man with a beard and shiny brown hair that hung in his face. He looked like an overstuffed bear with pudgy fingers and soft hands. He had buttonhole brown eyes that twinkled when he smiled, which he didn't do much of after Mrs. Hamilton introduced me.

"Heard anything?" Dave said.

Mrs. Hamilton shook her head, a tear rolling down her cheek.

Dave handed her a box of tissues and sat on the edge of his big desk. "I'm sure he'll turn up."

"How did you meet Larry?" I said, hoping he wouldn't think I was rude.

"Larry and I had a couple of college classes together, and we started hanging out, dreaming of starting a business. You should have seen some of the things we tried. Soap. Windshield cleaner. A salt-and-pepper dispenser that was the dumbest thing in the world." He looked at the floor and shook his head. "There's got to be an explanation. . . ."

CHAPTER 25

❀ Ashley ❀

Carolyn and I went outside to wait for our new clothes to arrive. We sat on a bench under the Huge BLOWOUT Sale! sign. At the top of the building another sign read No Interest for 12 Months. I knew what that meant, but it sounded like no one had been interested in the store for a year, and that made me smile.

I asked Carolyn about Tim. I felt bad that he and Bryce hadn't connected, but who could connect with Tim unless they wore a black trench coat and dyed their hair with shoe polish?

"It didn't happen that long ago," Carolyn said. "By the end of seventh grade he was hanging out with different kids. Then over the summer he changed his room, started listening to different music and staying out late. He fought with Mom and Dad about church—said they couldn't make him go. Guess he was right."

A brown van with the words *Lions and Tigers and Bears* painted on the side pulled up.

Oh, my.

A man emerged with two huge garment bags.

CHAPTER 26

◒ *Bryce* ◒

Larry Hamilton's floor was sectioned into two offices without doors so you could see the view 360 degrees. I could tell which office was Larry's because of all the Cubs stuff on the walls and the nameplate on his desk. Pretty smart detective for a kid, aren't I?

The windows were spotless, and I wondered who had the guts to walk out on the roof and clean them. Four floors looked like a long way down.

The bright-colored leaves left me speechless. That's one thing I miss about Illinois—all the leaves and trees. In Red Rock, it's mostly pine trees with a few aspens scattered around. Pine trees are okay in the winter with snow all over them, and I guess I should be glad we have trees that will grow in the dry climate, but it can get boring to see the same kind of tree everywhere you look.

I also saw a mom and a little boy throwing bits of bread to the ducks in a pond. It was something Mom would do with Dylan, and I suddenly missed them.

Larry's desk was pin neat. His Cubs pen was inserted into a crystal Cubs paperweight with a replica of Wrigley Field inside. When I shook it, baseballs swirled like snowflakes. Pennants hung on the wall, autographed baseballs sat encased in glass, and a Cubs clock ticked on the desk.

The message light on his phone blinked, and the readout said he had 31 messages. It killed me not to check them, but I figured Dave and the others wouldn't appreciate it and would probably do that themselves. I did scroll through the caller ID but didn't recognize any names.

I strolled back to Dave's office, trying not to look suspicious. He had a few Cubs things too but nothing like Larry's. Mostly Dave had pictures of people—some celebrities but most looked like family.

One picture was huge and grainy, showing Dave and Larry smiling and shaking hands over a document.

Dave said it was their original contract for the business. "You know, our agreement that we each own half the business. We both do about the same amount of work so it's fair."

"What happens if one of you dies?" I said.

Dave winced as if that was painful to even think about. "Dies? Wow." He shook his head. Finally he said, "The other person gets his share."

CHAPTER 27

❦ Ashley ❦

Granger may have liked both Carolyn and me, as her dad said, but for some reason he wanted to hide 95 percent of us inside costumes. Hers was a zebra and mine was a lion, and the only thing you could see of us was our faces. Had I come all this way to be an animal? Would I have to wear a tail on the path to Hollywood?

"People love animals and they love furniture," Granger said. "It's consistent with the image of the store, because they have a real lion in their newspaper ads."

The original commercial had Carolyn and me as sisters hoping our father would buy new furniture. "Wouldn't Mom love this?" Or

"Dad would really score points with the family with this couch, and it's on sale!" It was hokey but nothing embarrassing.

But the animal costumes crossed a line in the jungle. What if some of my old friends saw us?

"Hey, Sheila," I was supposed to say to the zebra, "nice furniture, huh?"

"Yeah," Sheila was to answer, "but some of these are spooky." At that point she was to walk past a black-and-white fake zebra chair, and the camera was to get a close-up of her face with her mouth open and eyes wide.

I was then to dramatically tell her how everything in the store was marked down, my tail swishing past patio furniture and bunk beds. At the end we were to come upon the real lion, have it roar, and then we would run through the parking lot hand in hand while the phone number was superimposed over our backsides.

If this was Granger's idea of helping us loosen up, I was glad I had to do it in a costume. Some kids might just take the money and not ask questions, but that's not me.

"What was wrong with the way we were before?" I said.

"Just not cute enough." Granger moved closer. "And if this works, I could see you two in a bunch of versions. Christmas. Valentine's Day. Memorial Day."

I could see Carolyn as a turkey and me a pumpkin pie, strolling through the furniture, the turkey telling me not to sit on anything.

CHAPTER 28

◕ *Bryce* ◕

On the train to Wrigley Field that afternoon, I watched the miles roll by and the outline of the city come into view. The Sears Tower stood like some army officer guarding the city.

I studied a newspaper, trying to seem interested in something so no one would ask if I was alone. I shouldn't have worried because hardly anyone even looked at me. I imagined myself moving back to Chicago someday, riding the train to Cubs games every summer afternoon, reading the *Chicago Tribune*, arguing with White Sox fans, and that kind of thing. I imagined so much that I nearly missed my stop. I hopped onto the platform just before the doors closed.

Crowds bustled and I suddenly realized how alone I was. I almost turned around. But I decided to pretend my dad was with me, that he hadn't died, hadn't been gone for years. "Nice day for a ball game," I said in my head to my dad.

"They should play two," my dad said.

"Ernie Banks!" I said. Dad said that was Ernie's famous line.

"Rootin' for the Cubbies?" a woman said behind me.

I turned and saw the perfect match for Larry. Every square inch of her outfit had something of the Cubs on it. I almost expected to see a red *C* on a tooth when she smiled.

I nodded. "My first game at Wrigley in a long time."

"Think they'll make the play-offs?" she said.

"Hope so."

"Me too." Then she launched into an analysis of the Cubs pitcher for the day and who he was up against. That led to her disgust with the manager and the lineup change he had made—or hadn't made, I couldn't tell which. For a Cubs fan she complained a lot, but I guess when you feel ownership in the team like she did, you have a right.

At the Addison Street station I stood at the railing and just looked at the ballpark. Tears stung my eyes as I remembered my dad taking me on that very train to a game against the Pittsburgh Pirates. I still have the scorecard in my room and have memorized the hits, the outs, who had home runs, the pitchers, everything.

At the ballpark I grabbed a scorecard from a vendor and headed for my standing-room-only spot.

CHAPTER 29

❀ Ashley ❀

I'd never felt more ridiculous in my life. No matter how tight I zipped, the lion's tail and rear end drooped. Carolyn's zebra was no better, and we both would have laughed if we hadn't been trying to keep from crying.

Granger pulled and rearranged the tails and actually used duct tape to make them fit better, but I wanted to shoot the "running through the parking lot" scene first and really do it.

"Can you imagine what Bryce will say?" I said.

"Just think of the money," Carolyn said.

"I don't care about the money anymore."

"Well, I do, so think of our friendship. If you walk out on me I'll never speak to you again."

I turned toward her. "Do you know how hard it is to take you seriously when you're wearing a zebra costume?"

That made her smile, and we started making zebra and lion jokes.

Granger returned while we were in slightly better moods. "Cute, cute, cute!" he said. "Cute squared. The viewers are going to be talking about this and flooding the store!"

Dustin had a hard time adjusting the lights to our costumes, complaining that our fur was too shiny, and that made us laugh more.

Mr. Hamilton left, saying he'd be back to pick us up later.

I guess it wouldn't have been half as bad if people hadn't shown up to watch. We were just two kids in costumes, sitting in overstuffed chairs, but you would have thought we were superstars.

"Is that anyone we know?" a woman whispered to her husband.

He held up a tag on a damaged dresser. "Don't think so."

Just as Dustin got his lighting right and was ready to roll on the first shot, Granger took a phone call.

"Relax," Dustin said. "He'll be back." He sat next to me. "Granger says you came all the way from Colorado to do this."

"Right. And I'm not wearing this home on the plane."

For the first time I noticed his smile. *He should be in front of the camera.* He was at least 15 years older than me, but a lioness can dream.

When the people watching saw there was nothing going on, they moved away. Dustin took some yellow tape from a desk and stretched it across the entrance. On it he wrote, *Quiet, filming in progress.* People would still be able to watch, just not as close.

"I'd be nervous with all those people staring." Dustin rubbed his eyes and leaned back on the couch. He had maybe a day's growth of beard and was wearing nice cologne. "Granger tells me your uncle is missing."

"The zebra's uncle," I said.

"Any word?" Dustin said.

"Nothing yet," Carolyn said. "I just hope something bad hasn't happened."

"Probably just jitters before the wedding," Dustin said.

CHAPTER 30

☻ *Bryce* ☻

I walked through the main entrance and up the steps to get my first view of the green grass, the scoreboard in the center, the white lines, and the ivy-covered fence. I could almost feel my dad's hand.

An usher herded me toward the standing-room-only area, a couple more ramps up.

I bought a bratwurst and something to drink, and it was so expensive I wished my dad could have paid for it. Still, with mustard and onions and ketchup, it tasted like a little bit of heaven.

The smells of a baseball game, as well as the sounds, are worth the price of admission. The popcorn, hot dogs, pizza, peanuts, cotton candy, and snow cones are enough to drive a hungry person crazy. But add the crack of the bat, the vendors, the laughter and excitement of the crowd, and you have a recipe for a great afternoon.

I must have looked at my watch a billion times, counting the minutes until the national anthem. I wrote down both lineups and took off my hat for the song, just like Dad. "Every time you hear this song," he'd said once, "remember there are men and women in places you would never want to live trying to keep us free enough to sing it. You honor them when you stand and take off your hat."

As the Cubs pitcher finished his warm-ups, I remembered Larry's seat number I'd written down. I dug it out and checked the section number. It was right below me and to the left in the Club Box seats.

I studied the numbers, locating the row and counting all the way down.

A guy in a floppy Cubs hat sat in Larry's seat.

❋ Ashley ❋

Granger returned and we walked through the first shot. Carolyn and I were to run a paw and a hoof over an oak desk with looks of awe. Then Carolyn was to say, "Wonder what the herd would say if I brought this home." My reaction was to nod and smile.

That took almost an hour, and we now had seven seconds finished. From there we moved to the bedroom furniture and finally to the end where we were supposed to see the real lion. I did my best to look afraid while Carolyn said, "My favorite section—where we get to eat!" Granger did a fake lion roar, and she said, "I said eat, not be eaten!"

It would be the lamest commercial in the history of television. I had the sinking feeling that if I did ever make it in the movies, someone would pull out this video on one of those late-night talk shows to make everybody laugh.

CHAPTER 32

◐ *Bryce* ◐

I kept one eye on the game and one on the guy in Larry Hamilton's seat. Was it Larry? Or someone who had kidnapped him and stolen his ticket?

The Cubs scored two runs in the bottom of the first, and the crowd went wild. By now, people stood behind and around me. Wrigley was full.

The Cubs pitcher had a no-hitter going in the fourth inning before a Cardinal smacked a ball into the basket in right field. The faithful fan who retrieved it tossed it back onto the field, and the crowd cheered. I love the Cubs, but I'm not sure I would have thrown the ball back.

By the fifth, my legs were tired, and I wondered if the guy in Larry's seat was ever going to head for the concession stand or the bathroom so I could get a look at him as he walked by.

Finally I gave up my place at the railing, walked down the ramp, and headed for the expensive seats. At every entrance an usher stood lookout, protecting seat holders from the railing riffraff.

A man with two kids came walking in with some drinks, and I still had mine in my hand. I edged closer and joined them, trying to look like part of their family. My heart beat like a drum as the usher smiled at the dad and the two kids. I was straining to see over them, watching the next pitch, when the usher put out his hand. "Ticket, please?"

I don't know why he asked for mine and not theirs—maybe he remembered them or something—but I just headed back toward the main entrance, watching the game on the concession-stand monitors. The Cubs scored a run in the bottom of the fifth on a single, a stolen base, a sacrifice bunt, and a long fly ball. It was beautiful.

I was thinking about going back to the railing when I overheard two guys in suits talking about having to leave. I'm not usually this brave, but I hurried to them before they made it outside and said, "Excuse me, sir, but I'm in standing room only and was wondering . . . if you're leaving, could I sit in your seat?"

The older guy looked at his friend. "Remember when we skipped school and came here?" He handed me his stub. "Knock yourself out, kid."

I studied the stub like it was the last golden Willy Wonka ticket. I expected light to engulf me and angels to sing.

It was a good section, right behind the Cubs dugout. I showed the usher, who looked like Count Olaf from the Lemony Snicket books, my ticket and climbed over a few people to get to the seat.

When I looked behind home plate for Larry's seat, the guy with the blue floppy hat wasn't there.

CHAPTER 33

✖ Ashley ✖

After lunch we went back inside for one more dining-room angle. Then came the final shot outside. It was the easiest because Carolyn and I just had to look scared and run. That felt weird. Why was a zebra teamed with a lion in the first place? Lions eat zebras.

"That's what makes it cute," Granger said. "A predator and the hunted teaming up to find furniture, and they meet another predator."

Mr. Hamilton returned and caught Carolyn and me lounging on a couch. His face looked tight, like someone had punched him in the stomach.

"News about Uncle Larry?" Carolyn said.

Mr. Hamilton bit his cheek. "Yeah, the police found his car at the airport. It doesn't look good."

CHAPTER 34

☻ *Bryce* ☻

It's one thing to see a ball thrown on TV but another to watch it yourself and hear the pop of the catcher's mitt. The pitcher was throwing so hard that you could almost see smoke coming from the ball.

Floppy Hat still wasn't back, but I was enjoying my new seat, free from the scrutiny of ushers. The people around me seemed like regulars, talking and joking. There was nervous laughter as the Cardinals got a couple of back-to-back hits, then a walk that loaded the bases.

"Come on, you bum—throw strikes!" a guy behind me yelled.

The count was 2–0 when the Cardinals hitter connected with a blast to left field. There was no doubt it was destined for Waveland Avenue. Four runs with one swing, and suddenly the Cubs were behind.

The guy behind me cursed the pitcher, and an older man in front of me turned and told him to watch his language. Then another younger guy started jawing with him, and when the Cubs manager walked onto the field, the guy with the foul mouth yelled louder.

"Can't you see we've got kids here?" the older man said.

"Kids shouldn't be allowed to see this slaughter," the guy said, tacking on a few more choice words.

I counted five empty beer cups at the man's feet, and he held another full cup. His face was red, his eyes glassy.

Someone brought an usher. The blue-vested man asked the guy to calm down, but that just got him more riled. The usher called Security, and suddenly things got interesting.

"I've been coming to games for more than 30 years, and I've never been kicked out," the guy slurred.

A black man with arms the size of tree trunks came down the stairs, followed by a white guy with arms the size of telephone poles and a neck the size of a fire hydrant. They waved for the guy to follow them, but it was clear he didn't want to.

"I'll be quiet now, okay? I'll be a good boy and not disturb the innocent ears around here. Okay? Okay?"

The two security guys had the people in the row stand and walk to the aisle. As soon as the guy moved away from them, two more security guys showed up at the other end. The guy tried to move back to his seat but lost his balance, then tried to catch himself on my row. His drink went flying, and before I could react I was covered in warm Budweiser.

"Now look what you did," the guy hollered. "You made me spill on this fine young man."

The tree trunks and telephone poles converged and pulled the guy up the stairs.

People clapped.

An usher handed me a towel. "We're sorry about this," he said.

I wondered what Mrs. Hamilton would think when I came home smelling like a brewery.

In the midst of the commotion I spotted Floppy Hat. He had returned to his seat, his hat pulled low.

The usher gave me a free Cubs T-shirt as the crowd reacted to the Cardinals' final out of the inning.

Floppy Hat was clapping.

CHAPTER 35

❀ Ashley ❀

As we drove home, Mr. Hamilton turned on the radio, and we listened to the seventh-inning stretch of the Cubs game. With the Cubs behind, the celebrity singing "Take Me Out to the Ball Game" yelled, "Let's get some runs!"

A news guy came on the radio with headlines, including one about a "runaway groom" in Ridgefield. Of course we knew who he was talking about.

"I wonder how the newspeople found out," Carolyn said.

Mr. Hamilton switched to an all-news station.

Within five minutes we heard the report: "Authorities say they have no leads regarding a missing Ridgefield man who was to be married Saturday. Entrepreneur Larry Hamilton was last seen by friends Monday, and today authorities discovered his car at O'Hare International Airport. Any information on his whereabouts should be directed to the Ridgefield police department."

CHAPTER 36

☺ *Bryce* ☺

My cell phone rang.

"Are you at the game?" Mom said.

"I'm so sorry I forgot to call, Mom. I got caught up in the game and everything and—"

"I was just sitting here watching and wondering where you were sitting."

I told her while keeping an eye on Floppy Hat. I thought about walking over to Floppy Hat and getting a closer look at him, but I told myself I'd wait until the middle of the eighth and pretend to have dropped something over there. I thanked Mom for calling and said Ashley and I were having a good time. She said she missed us.

At the end of the seventh Floppy Hat joined a throng headed for the stairs. Was he going to the bathroom? the concessions stand? outside?

I had to find out.

My heart sank as I got to the stairs. Floppy Hat exited the front. If I followed, I wouldn't be allowed back inside and would miss the rest of the game. But if I didn't, I'd never know who this guy was.

I ran through the abandoned turnstiles and followed him to Addison Street.

CHAPTER 37

❀ Ashley ❀

Mrs. Hamilton absently asked how the commercial had gone, and when Carolyn said it had been a disaster, she said, "That's nice."

The phone rang and Mr. Hamilton answered. His face fell. He told his wife, "One of Larry's neighbors says there're a couple of TV trucks at Larry's house."

The phone rang again.

"Reporters have been calling all afternoon," Mrs. Hamilton said. "They're asking for photos of Larry."

Carolyn pulled me upstairs. "This is getting weird. I'm sorry you had to be here for this."

"It's not your fault," I said. "How were you supposed to know this was going to happen?"

I heard the familiar rumble of music blasting from a car. School was out, and the streets were filled with rowdy drivers loosed for the day. I looked out the window and saw Tim get out of a black car. At least six people were squeezed into the thing. The driver had jet-black hair with purple highlights.

Someone threw Tim's backpack to him through the window.

"Don't forget, Saturday night," the driver hollered.

Carolyn opened the door to Mrs. Hamilton's knock. "Granger just called. The store owner wants something reshot tonight at around 10."

I closed my eyes at the thought of putting on that costume again. Being in a furniture commercial was not as glamorous as it had sounded.

Carolyn left for a minute, so I sat on her bed and looked out the window. The tree outside reminded me of one at our old house, and I realized I hadn't visited like I'd promised Mom.

Tim walked by and I asked how he was doing. He just scowled.

"What's going on Saturday night?" I said.

He stopped and narrowed his eyes at me. "I don't spy on you and your brother."

"I didn't mean to—"

"Just keep it to yourself, okay?"

CHAPTER 38

○ *Bryce* ○

I scanned the crowd outside Wrigley, but there was no Floppy Hat in sight. Buses lined Addison Street, and police officers directed traffic. The L train clattered to a stop behind me, and I suddenly felt even more alone.

Already a huge crowd waited to cross Clark Street—people who either had better things to do or had given up on the Cubbies. I hadn't given up on them. I just had a job to do.

That's when I saw Floppy Hat passing street vendors hawking peanuts, water, shirts, and hats. I took off, clutching my new T-shirt like it was a million-dollar bill.

A kid holding her father's hand gave me a mean look and held her nose as I passed. I raced past them and reached the sidewalk, keeping an eye on Floppy Hat three blocks away. I ran past grizzled old men selling Cubs stuffed animals and inflatable bats. How long had these people waited for a winner? Or did losing for so long draw even more fans?

I heard a roar from the stadium, always a beautiful sound. Radios blared from makeshift shacks, and I heard "RBI single."

Floppy Hat was heavy and pigeon-toed—his feet pointing at each other as he walked. He wiped sweat from his brow with a handkerchief and took off his hat to fan himself.

I had pulled within a block of him when he turned right and disappeared. I struggled to catch up. The air was thick and muggy, and my shirt stuck to my back. The drying beer made me not even want to be around myself.

I passed a few teenagers who laughed and called to me. I kept going as if I didn't hear them.

When I turned the corner the guy was nowhere in sight. I had run half a block when I heard an engine start. A shiny car that looked like a tank idled in the driveway of an old house. Floppy Hat removed something from his dashboard.

I waved and yelled, but the guy didn't hear me.

The teenagers mimicked me, waving and running toward me. Not a good sign.

Floppy Hat pulled into the street. He turned the other way, and I tried to get his attention. I got a good look at his license plate.

"Kid!" someone yelled. "Let's see your shirt!"

CHAPTER 39

✖ Ashley ✖

Carolyn said she needed to talk with her mother, so I went for a walk. I should have known when they hadn't picked Bryce and me up at the airport that things were going to get squirrelly. How squirrelly was still a mystery.

I walked past houses I'd known as a child. They seemed smaller, closer together, like everything else on this trip. Funny how things seem to change as you get older.

Mr. Mondesi's driveway was still filled with cars. He fixed them in his spare time, and there were always oil stains on his concrete.

The hedges around Mrs. Kramer's yard were greener and fuller than ever. Her little black dog, Zip, sniffed at the fence and barked. I had watched him while she and her husband had been away on vacation once, even though I was just a kid. Mr. Kramer had died before we moved, and it was really sad.

At the end of the street our house sat on a little hill. The crab-apple tree in front was full of leaves, and the oak tree next to it flamed orange and red and yellow. I could barely see the front door and windows, but the garage door was straight ahead.

Then I saw our old mailbox. My dad had painted the whole thing black and sunk it in the ground with a bunch of concrete. Bryce and I had written our names in it before it dried, but now it had chipped away so all you could see was *yce & Ashl.* I ran my hand across the letters.

Sometimes I feel like we've lived in Colorado all our lives and my old life never really happened, that we never lived in Ridgefield, never had a dad other than Sam. Things would be a lot simpler if that were true.

About 50 yards from our house sat a little park with a slide and swings. Bryce and I had thought we were so grown-up when we walked there alone. Now there was a new teeter-totter, monkey bars, and lots of other equipment. Instead of pea gravel, the tiny rocks that get in your shoes and drive you crazy, they'd put down some rubber stuff in different colors. I wished we'd had such a nice park, but part of me missed the old one.

Across the field behind our house sat the library. How many trips had we made to get a book on tape or go to story time? In the summer they showed movies in the basement—tickets were free and most of the movies had been on video for at least a year, but we felt like kings and queens in that cool room, stretching out on beanbags.

Our old swing set still stood in the backyard and so did our shed, though the new owners had painted it green. Now there was a picnic table on the patio and a hot tub just outside the sliding-glass door. Pippin had run in that yard and this field. We'd played football here and hit golf balls. Once the drainage grate had gotten stuck with debris and the place flooded. It rose almost to our backyard, and Bryce and I bobbed around in our rubber boat.

A thousand memories—good ones—flooded me now. Flying kites. Playing flashlight tag. Sleeping in a tent in the backyard. Wiffle-ball games.

I walked into our old yard and sat in one of the swings, running my hands up and down the rusted chains. Bright leaves above me spread like a rainbow canopy. The world and its problems melted away, and I thought only of what it felt like to be home.

I noticed a bump in the sand. I knelt and scraped until I uncovered a metal headlight from an old Hot Wheels car—something Bryce had left behind. I dusted it off. It was like digging up an artifact from our former life, and it made me want to bring Bryce to look for more relics.

I quickly looked up when the back door opened.

"Can I help you?" a woman said.

CHAPTER 40

☻ *Bryce* ☻

There are times when you feel like God is watching out for
you. This wasn't one of them.

I'd heard about kids getting jumped by gangs. Still, there was no
way I was giving up my shirt, and as the kids ran toward me, I raced
up the sidewalk to the other side of the street.

The kids cursed me, and that's when the screen door opened to
the house where Floppy Hat had parked. An old man came out, and
I heard the Cubs game from inside.

"What's going on out here?" he shouted.

"Those guys are after me," I said, pointing and short of breath.

"You hooligans get out of here before I call the cops!" he hollered.

I bent over, hands on knees, and looked back.

The kids retreated.

"What did you do to them?"

"Nothing. I just ran past them." I held out the shirt. "I think they wanted this."

"Nice. You get it at the game?"

I nodded. "I was trying to catch up to the guy who was parked here. You know who he is?"

"Larry? Yeah, he parks here for every game."

"Did you see him today?" I said.

"No, can't say that I did."

"Anyone else ever park here?"

"Just the people Larry lets have tickets. Guess it could have been one of them."

Down the street the kids still watched me. I knew better than to go into a stranger's house, but I had to do something. "I can't get back into the game. Mind if I sit on your porch and listen?"

The man scowled. "Go home, kid."

CHAPTER 41

❧ Ashley ❧

"I'm sorry. I used to live here," I said, hoping the woman wouldn't call the police.

The woman moved toward me, her head cocked. "Are you Ashley?"

When I nodded, she smiled. "So many things around here had your name on them. We found it carved in one of the upstairs closets. The neighborhood still talks about you and your family."

She reached for the Hot Wheels car and examined it. "This has to be your brother's, because we don't have boys."

"Probably," I said, relieved she wasn't upset.

"I'll bet you'd like to look around inside."

"Sure it'd be okay?"

She walked me to the back door.

I stopped at the step into the kitchen, took a breath, and slipped off my sandals. "It's been a long time."

I've read that you can never go home again, but I didn't understand it until now. This was like stepping back into one of Mom's Creative Memories books, only it was someone else's memory.

There were new window treatments throughout, new carpet in the living room, great black-and-white family photos on the walls, and flowers and plants all over. My room had been painted a soft yellow, and the bed had a canopy—something I had dreamed about.

"My oldest daughter enjoys this room when she's home from college," the woman said. "Take a look at your brother's room."

Bryce would have tossed his Pop-Tarts. The walls were pink, posters of music stars hung everywhere, and a birdcage in the corner housed two cute finches. They flitted about the cage and squeaked.

I found out this was her 17-year-old's room. She had two girls—one in college, and the other a senior in high school who worked at the local Blockbuster.

They'd redone the bathroom, the master bedroom, and even the garage. It looked like the people from *Extreme Makeover: Home Edition* had been here.

I kicked myself for not bringing my camera, and the woman said she could take some pictures of me and send them. She shot me in my old room, outside on the swings, by the hot tub, and at the front door. She also said I could bring Bryce by so he could take a look.

"The neighbors told me what happened to your father," the woman said. "I'm so sorry." She said it like she really meant it.

My throat closed. "Yeah, me too. I like it in Colorado and we have a really good stepdad, but I'd give anything to have our real dad back."

CHAPTER 42

☽ *Bryce* ☽

The old man letting the screen door close in my face was like a dagger in my chest. I prayed God would send lightning bolts to the kids behind me.

When I turned, two of them ran toward me. The other two weren't in sight. *Great. They've divided so they can conquer.*

I hopped the small fence that ran around the man's yard. At the back stood another fence, this one a little taller. I got over and raced for the next street. I darted past a window in the next house, and a dog the size of a truck barked through the screen. I almost left my bratwurst on the grass, but I made it to the street.

I turned left and ran hard, but the guys behind me yelled, "We're going to get you! You're dead!" They didn't know I was from high altitude. They say that if an athlete trains at a higher elevation, then comes to a lower elevation, he has a huge edge. His lungs have been trained to get by on half the oxygen, so when he runs at sea level he has a ton of endurance.

Unfortunately, the guys behind me had longer legs, and the two coming down the alley looked like they'd eaten double bowls of Wheaties.

I turned right and ran west like I'd never run before, but they were gaining on me. My heart pounded, I was out of breath, and I almost dropped my shirt in the street.

Then I spotted a blue-and-white cruiser that said *We Serve and Protect* on the side. A police officer stood with his foot on the bumper of a car, writing something.

"Hey!"

The guys behind me pulled up, sneering and jeering. Two others joined them, and they looked at me like I was a rabbit that had gotten away.

"Problem?" the officer said.

I put my hands on my knees and let the sweat drip from my nose. "Those guys were after me," I said, gasping. "I think they wanted my shirt."

He kept writing as I caught my breath. Then I told him where I was from and that I was scared to go back to the L alone.

"Hop in, kid."

CHAPTER 43

❀ Ashley ❀

I walked back to the Hamiltons' with thoughts of how things used to be flooding my mind. I forced myself back to the present and to the mystery at hand.

I noticed movement in an upstairs window and saw Tim on a cell phone, pacing. He looked out and gave me a blank stare.

Carolyn came out. "We've been looking for you, Ashley. Your brother called. Said it was urgent."

I went in and called him. His phone cut in and out, and there was a lot of noise in the background. I realized he was on the train.

"Ashley, you won't believe what happened."

He told me the whole story and said the policeman who gave him a ride to the L also ran the license number Bryce had seen through the system.

"It's registered to a Tucker Brooks of Ridgefield, but I didn't recognize the street."

I told him I had to go back to the furniture store late to finish the commercial shoot and promised I wouldn't say anything to the Hamiltons until he got back.

When I hung up Tim was behind me.

"What did your brother say?"

"Said he had a good time."

He cocked his head. "Really?"

I nodded and tried to smile.

CHAPTER 44

◔ *Bryce* ◔

I got weird stares on the train because of my beer-soaked shirt. When I switched trains to head west, I found out from a guy with headphones that the game had gone into extra innings, and the Cubs pulled it out in the bottom of the 11th.

Mrs. Hamilton was sitting tight-faced in the parking lot with Ashley when I got off the train. I took the front seat and glanced back. Ashley had a look like she was about to explode. I knew if I didn't tell Mrs. Hamilton what I had learned, Ashley would.

Mrs. Hamilton said if it was okay she needed to stop at Larry's office to speak with Peggy. I asked if she knew anyone named Tucker Brooks.

"Of course. He works with Larry. A real computer whiz. Why?"

"Oh, ah, I just wanted to talk to him about . . . computers."

"Tucker and Larry don't see eye to eye on everything," she said, "but I think they're at a good place now."

"What was the problem?" Ashley said.

"Just differences of opinion about where the company should go. Whether they should sell. That kind of thing. I think they've worked through it."

When we pulled into the parking lot, I immediately recognized Tucker's car, and there was a blue floppy hat on the passenger seat.

Mrs. Hamilton showed us where Tucker's office was and went to find Peggy.

Ashley grabbed my arm as I was about to knock. "You sure you know what you're doing?" she whispered.

"It'll be okay," I said. "I won't let him know I saw him today."

I knocked.

A voice like Darth Vader's said, "Come in."

CHAPTER 45

�֎ Ashley �֎

Tucker sat behind a Super Big Gulp. He had short brown hair, eyebrows that needed plucking, and lips half the women in Hollywood would have paid for. He looked like a computer geek, and I wanted to tell him pleats were out and made him look heavier, but I held back.

I told him we were friends of the Hamiltons.

"Here for the wedding?" he said, his voice booming like the guy in the movie commercials. But as he said it something must have clicked in his brain. His eyes flickered, like his monitor had finally powered up. "Timberline, right? You're the ones whose father...?"

"Yeah, that's us," I said.

"I'm really sorry you went through that. I remember the articles in the paper."

I looked around the office for a clue—a piece of rope, a bloody knife, a suitcase full of cash, or a book titled *How to Kidnap Your Boss for Fun and Profit.*

A picture of Peggy and Tucker in the corner made me wonder if Tucker could be in love with her and had done something to get Larry out of the way.

Other than the pictures, all that decorated the walls was Cubs and Bears memorabilia. I wondered if you had to be a sports nut to get a job here.

"So you like the Cubs," Bryce said.

Tucker smiled. "They're still in it. Won a thriller today."

I leaned on the desk and sighed. "Wouldn't you have just loved to be there? All that excitement."

Bryce and I studied the guy like an algebra problem.

"Actually," he said, "I *was.*"

"I heard it was standing room only," Bryce said. "How'd you get a ticket?"

Tucker laced his fingers behind his head and leaned back in his chair. "On Sunday Larry told me he wasn't going to be able to go, so he gave me his ticket and parking directions."

"You tell the police that?" Bryce said.

He shook his head. "Didn't think it was important."

"Why couldn't he go?" Bryce said. "This was one of the most important games of the year. He wouldn't miss that for anything, would he?"

"Not usually, and he seemed sad handing me the ticket and his parking pass. There have been other times when he couldn't go, and he'd always offer me the chance. . . ."

"I hear you and Larry have had problems," I said.

He nodded. "But it's always been creative tension. You know, get talented people together and they'll disagree. We've always known we're on the same team, though."

"So why couldn't he go to the game?" Bryce said. "What did he tell you?"

Tucker put his hands together. "You think *I'm* somehow involved?"

"Are you?" Bryce said.

"I don't need kids nosing around. Get out of my office."

CHAPTER 46

◎ *Bryce* ◎

We had to wonder if the police had found Tucker's finger-
prints in Larry Hamilton's car at the airport.

Ashley said she thought Mr. Hamilton was acting funny, but I
thought that might be his way of handling bad news.

"What about Peggy?" I said. "You know from past mysteries that
it can sometimes be the last person you'd think of."

Ashley made a face. "Are you listening to the woman sob?"

"Maybe that's from remorse—you know, that she did something
bad to Larry. Maybe he's already taken out the life-insurance policy,
and she knew that."

Ashley rolled her eyes. "Now you're just being silly. I can tell Peggy loves Larry. She's supposed to be walking down the aisle Saturday, and they can't find the guy who gave her the ring."

"I'm just saying we should look at all the angles."

Ashley told me about her visit to our old house and said that I could come by before we left on Monday. I wasn't sure I wanted to, with all the memories being kicked up at Wrigley and around the neighborhood. I had a feeling that if I went to the middle school I'd see more friends who would open old wounds.

Like Tina Workman. I'd known her since first grade. Part of me hoped I'd see her. Another part hoped I wouldn't.

I went to the water fountain, and when I came back Peggy and Mrs. Hamilton were embracing, both of them holding tissues and wiping their eyes.

CHAPTER 47

❀ Ashley ❀

Bryce said he'd go with us to the furniture store, and Mr. Hamilton stopped by Dairy Queen on the way. It had been one of our favorite things to do with our dad—ride bikes through some back streets, eat our ice cream (Reese's Peanut Butter Cup Blizzard is my favorite), then ride to a park and watch the sunset. Compared with Colorado, Illinois sunsets are tame, but we didn't know that back then. The sun goes down over cornfields or trees, and the whole thing makes you hungry for an ocean or mountain scene.

Mr. Hamilton asked Bryce about the game, and Bryce told him. I knew there was more to the story than the runs, hits, and errors, but Bryce stuck to the stats. For some reason he didn't want anyone else knowing he'd seen Tucker at the game. He told me it was a good sign that Tucker had admitted being there, but we were both suspicious.

We got to the furniture store at about nine, and Carolyn and I went into the ladies' room to change into our costumes. All of our shots would be inside and mostly close-ups of us looking at each other and reacting to what the other said.

We went into the manager's office and waited, hoping no one would see us.

Granger came in and went over a couple of shots we'd be doing through the store after all the customers were out. We were supposed to prowl through the couches and easy chairs. Just something they could put in the background that would look interesting, I guess.

When Granger finished, I said, "It's too bad about Mr. Hamilton's brother, isn't it?"

Granger got a weird look on his face. "What do you mean?"

"Carolyn's uncle," I said. "He's missing."

"Larry Hamilton? That's your father's brother?" His mouth dropped. "I just saw that on the news this evening. Any idea what happened?"

Carolyn told him, but something felt funny. Dustin had said Granger had told him about Larry. Was Granger lying?

When he left us alone, I walked through the store to the parking lot and found Bryce. I explained the discrepancy and asked him to look into it.

"What do you want me to do, go through his car?" Bryce said.

"Hadn't thought of that," I said. "Not a bad idea."

CHAPTER 48

☺ *Bryce* ☺

At 10, the store closed its doors and I stayed outside. Customers walked to their cars, talking about the cost of chairs or bedroom sets, where they'd get the money, what good credit terms the store had. I still don't understand credit—Sam says if you don't want to get in trouble with money you shouldn't buy anything you can't pay for.

Mr. Hamilton said he had to go somewhere, which left me alone with the employees' cars, Granger's van, and about a billion fluorescent lights. Moths fluttered around them like fans at a concert, but as night came, a chilly wind blew. When the last employees came out and locked the door, I knew I was alone.

I'd seen Granger and Dustin drive up in the van, and Granger told me he'd leave it unlocked if I wanted to stay outside. I climbed in the passenger side and carefully took out the contents of the glove compartment. I found a leather pouch with the registration and proof of insurance. There was also a manual on how to work the radio, some fuses, and receipts from an oil-change place. I put it all back neatly, just the way I'd found it.

I looked under the seats and found some uneaten French fries, a few cracked Doritos, and a hotel pen. No sign of Larry under there. In the captain chairs (and between them) were Dustin's equipment boxes and some tripods. I looked behind the backseat and found jumper cables. I sat in one of the captain chairs and wondered what connection Granger could possibly have had to Larry.

That's when I noticed a leather bag wedged next to the driver's seat. It almost looked like a purse, but when I opened it, I found a thin laptop that I could tell was pretty new and screaming fast. There were CDs and DVDs in a pouch—I guess pictures or videos of some commercials—and some papers.

I put the computer back and was about to zip the pouch when I spotted a page or two of a folded newspaper in the side pocket. It was the announcement page from the local *Ridgefield Guardian*, complete with pictures of couples about to be married or who had gotten engaged.

One entry was circled.

> *Robert and Margerite Murphy of Ridgefield announce the engagement of their daughter, Sara Christine Murphy, to Anthony Michael Trainor, son of Bill and Lois Trainor of Des Plaines.*

The article went on to say where Sara and Anthony had graduated from college, listed their degrees, where they worked, and where and when the wedding would be held, which was in about six months.

I took out the hotel pen I had found and wrote the names down. The name *Murphy* seemed familiar, but I couldn't place it. Why was the announcement circled? Was Granger doing wedding productions? Did this have anything to do with Larry? Was I on a wild-goose chase when the real culprit worked right in Larry's own office?

The side door slid open, and Dustin stood in the fluorescent light, with furrowed brow. "Find anything interesting?"

I let the newspaper fall to the floor. "I'm Bryce, Ashley's brother. I was just . . ." I couldn't think of anything to say, and as he dug into his camera gear, I guessed it didn't matter.

"No problem here," Dustin said. "Not my van."

PART 4

CHAPTER 49

FRIDAY

❋ Ashley ❋

I awoke to a *tap-tap-tap* and thought someone was trying to get into our room. It was just raindrops pattering Carolyn's window. The sky was as gray as . . . something really gray. Dark, overcast, puddles on the sidewalk, windshield wipers whipping back and forth on the passing cars.

A truly great day.

You see, in Colorado we get rain, but the sun usually comes back out and brightens up the world and dries up all the water. I like the sun, don't get me wrong, but sometimes it's nice to have a day that's yucky to make you appreciate the really good days.

Carolyn wasn't in the room so I lay back on my pillow and stretched. It felt like years since I'd slept in my own bed, and I had an ache in my heart to see Mom and tell her all that had happened. I knew it was an hour earlier in Colorado, and there was no way I was going to wake her and the rest of the family, even though it would have been kind of fun to wake Leigh up.

The shoot the night before had gone okay. We'd stalked through the store like good little lions and zebras, but I had the sinking feeling this wouldn't lead to bigger things.

The one interesting thing that came out of the night was Bryce's discovery in Granger's van. We found the newspaper announcement in the recycle bin in the Hamiltons' garage and cut out the picture. The name *Murphy* sounded familiar to me too, but I couldn't remember where I'd heard it.

Carolyn came back with a huge cinnamon roll and some eggs, along with a tall glass of orange juice. "Breakfast in bed," she said. "Bryce is already dressed."

"Good for him."

"Gonna be kind of wet today so Mom said she'd drive us. Have you decided what you're going to do?"

"I'll probably stick with Bryce and Tim."

"Not Freddie?" Carolyn laughed.

I tried to get her mind off boys, but it was a constant theme with her. Ever since I'd been here she'd brought up boyfriends and weird stuff about the guys she knew. I guess high school will do that, but it made me uncomfortable. I asked if she'd heard anything about her uncle.

She stopped laughing and sat on the bed. "There's no news, which is really bad. Since they found his car, they think something's happened to him. They're sure now he didn't get on a plane."

"Who would have taken his car to the airport? He sounds like such a nice guy. Why would anyone want to hurt him?"

"Dad says we may never know."

CHAPTER 50

◔ *Bryce* ◔

The situation with Carolyn's uncle Larry made me want
to skip school and concentrate on that, but part of me wanted to go
back and see my old friends, and Mrs. Hamilton had gone to a lot of
trouble to get Ashley and me in.

Part of me also felt in over my head with the mystery. We didn't
have transportation like at home. No ATVs to ride on the streets of
Ridgefield. Plus, the town had changed so much in the years since
we had left, and we were dealing with an adult world. All that
mixed together made it even more of a challenge—our most difficult test yet.

I caught Mr. Hamilton before he left for work and asked about Granger. He said he hadn't known the man long, that they'd worked on some commercials, but that was it. Then I asked about Tucker.

Mr. Hamilton's face grew tight. "I have my suspicions about him. Larry's had problems with him since they started working together." He looked around the room and lowered his voice, like he didn't want his wife hearing. "I told the police something that happened about a year ago, and they're looking into it."

"What happened?"

"Larry and Tucker had a disagreement about the Web site—Larry didn't like the look and asked my opinion. I agreed with him. Well, Tucker found out that Larry had shown his work to somebody outside the company, and he went ballistic."

"What did he do?"

"Threw a paperweight and made a hole in the wall. Tossed a desk. There was probably more to it than just me looking at the site, but the point is that Tucker is capable of doing stupid things."

"You think he'd hurt Larry?"

"He threatened to kill him once. Now I don't know if that was just something he said in anger or if he really meant it, but the police thought it was important."

"Has anything happened in the last few weeks to make Tucker mad?"

Mr. Hamilton shook his head. "Not that I know of. Larry said they'd been working well together. But with somebody like Tucker, it only takes one little thing to set him off."

I was about to tell Mr. Hamilton about what I'd seen at the Cubs game, but his cell phone rang and the next minute he was out the door.

CHAPTER 51

✖ Ashley ✖

Ridgefield Middle School has to be the oldest school on earth. The sidewalks look like they've been through an earthquake. The bricks are crumbling. The floors squeak. A tornado years before had torn up the sports fields and nearby houses and businesses. Everything was ripped apart except the school.

I was a stranger to most of these students. I recognized a face here or there, but most had their heads down as they moved from class to class.

Tim wasn't interested in being with us, so Bryce called his friend Taylor and went with him. At the last minute, Jill Paulson (I knew her from dance class in second grade) asked if I wanted to hang with her.

Jill's first period was algebra, which I thought cruel. I noticed Freddie in the corner with his arms crossed, and my heart skipped a beat.

He raised his eyebrows and said, "Ashley?"

We had a good time talking. Things had changed a lot since we had chased each other on the playground (like him growing up and becoming so cute), but it felt like old times.

"You moving back?" he said.

I shook my head. "We like Colorado, and our stepdad has a good job. He's a charter pilot."

"Cool. Maybe I can come out there sometime."

The teacher came in and I sat near Jill. I kept looking over and catching Freddie looking at me. (Maybe moving back wasn't such a bad idea.) The next time I peeked at him, Freddie was sitting back with his eyes closed. I wondered if he'd been up late talking to his girlfriend.

With announcements over the loudspeaker came the list of the day's birthdays, including Bridgette Murphy's. The name finally clicked. Sara Murphy had been our babysitter once, and she'd brought Bridgette with her. Bridgette was our age and had more energy than a superhero. She had curly blonde hair and a petite gymnast's figure. At least she did when she was little.

"Have any classes with Bridgette, Jill?" I said.

"Sure, third period."

CHAPTER 52

☺ *Bryce* ☺

Taylor was in band, and the teacher let me join the percussion section. I knew a few kids, and several girls kept turning and staring at me, then whispering. Made me feel like a fish in a bowl.

After class one girl came and asked if I was the kid whose dad died in a plane crash. It wasn't very sensitive, but you had to admit she had, as Huck Finn would say, a lot of sand.

Taylor had shop class next, and it was cool because they were making their own pens out of wood, then carving and finishing holders for them that looked like a million bucks. I had never thought of shop class before, but I promised myself I'd try it next semester.

We were headed to third period when we passed a trophy case where broken glass was held together with duct tape.

"What happened?" I said.

Taylor shook his head. "Nothing compared to what happened at the high school. The place has been vandalized five times since school started. They put a security guard there. Then we got trashed."

CHAPTER 53

✿ Ashley ✿

Bridgette Murphy hadn't grown much—she was lucky to hit four feet—but she made up for it in muscle and pigtails. Her posture was perfect, and just watching her walk made me think of those poised gymnasts in the Olympics.

She was all smiles, and she said she remembered playing at our house. "I'm so sorry about your dad."

That event had come to define me. I was the girl whose dad died in a plane crash, a person to be pitied.

The truth was, I hadn't gotten over it, but with help I didn't think of it every moment. I didn't cry myself to sleep, didn't lock my door

and push people away. In fact, coming back here was actually helping me deal with lots of memories.

"I saw the announcement in the paper about your sister. Is she
the one who babysat us?"

Bridgette gave me a pained smile. "Yes. But the wedding is kind
of on hold."

"Really? They looked so happy in the picture."

"They are. I think they'll still get married, but maybe not that
soon."

"If you don't mind my asking, what's the problem?"

She bit her cheek. "It's the weirdest thing. Sara and her fiancé
were laughing and having a great time. He leaves the house, the
phone rings, and she starts crying. Next thing I know the wedding's
been called off and we can't get my sister to come out of her room."

"Did Sara have everything booked for the wedding?" I said. "A
photographer or videographer? Someone to record the ceremony?"

Bridgette frowned. "I don't think they got that far. She didn't
even have her dress yet, just the church."

CHAPTER 54

◖ *Bryce* ◗

I remembered Bridgette because I used to call her Bridgette the Midget and make her cry.

"What are you smiling about?" Ashley said.

"Nothing."

"Seems like an awful lot of weddings are getting interrupted around here," she said.

"Why don't we take the rest of the day off and do some investigating?" I said.

Mrs. Hamilton came and got us, and when we apologized for not sticking with the plan, she said, "After what we put you through at the airport, it's no problem. You're here to have fun."

Back at the house I found the number for Granger's company and used my cell phone. The caller ID would show my Colorado number. When a woman answered, I deepened my voice. "I was wondering if your company does wedding videos."

"No, sir, we're a commercial firm, but I can give you a referral if you'd like."

I told her that wouldn't be necessary, then told Ashley.

"So why did Granger have that couple's picture circled?" she said.

"Maybe we're concentrating on the wrong person," I said. "Every clue so far points to Tucker."

CHAPTER 55

❀ Ashley ❀

Bryce and I wrote down everything we knew about Larry and those he worked with. We asked Mrs. Hamilton about places Larry went, and mostly it was work, out with Peggy, or to church.

First Church of Ridgefield was about a mile from the Hamiltons' house. It wasn't large—it actually looked more like a recreation center. A sign in front said "Work like it's all up to you. Pray like it's all up to God."

There was one car in the parking lot, so Bryce and I banged on the door. I felt like the persistent widow in one of Jesus' parables.

A man finally opened the door. "Can I help you?"

We said we were looking for the pastor, and the man said, "You're looking at him."

When we told him who we were, he said, "You're the kids whose dad . . ."

He led us inside, and we told him we were trying to help find Larry Hamilton.

"I've told the police everything I know," he said. "The congregation is sick about it. We had a special prayer meeting last night."

"Do you know Tucker Brooks?" Bryce said.

The pastor looked hard at us. "When Larry was starting his business he came to me about Tucker. Larry was concerned that if he entered into a business relationship with an unbeliever, that could make things difficult. I told him he was right, that 2 Corinthians 6 spoke to that very issue. Larry eventually decided to go ahead. He thought he might be able to talk to Tucker about God."

"Did he?" Bryce said.

The pastor winced. "Yes and no. Tucker wanted Larry to leave him alone, to not push the Bible down his throat, that kind of thing. They have a lot of things in common, but the Lord is not one of them."

"Do you think Tucker did something to him?" I said.

The pastor paused, then said, "I don't know what to think. Larry is as solid a man as you'll ever find. Not flighty. Predictable. If he says he'll be some place, he'll be there. If he makes a commitment, he follows through."

"Like a wedding," I said.

"Exactly. But last weekend he didn't seem himself. He was distracted at our deacon/elder meeting. I thought it was because of the wedding. Everyone joked with him about it, saying he had only a few days of freedom left. But afterward, he said he needed to talk.

I asked if we could have breakfast the next morning. He said yes but never showed up. I left a message on his phone, then went by his office. I keep thinking if I'd just talked with him after the meeting, he wouldn't have disappeared."

CHAPTER 56

☺ *Bryce* ☺

While on our way back from the church, Ashley and I saw dark clouds rise in the west, so we picked up our pace. The wind bending the trees and turning up the leaves brought back memories of huddling under the stairs at home, afraid of a tornado. One time our dad had gone outside and stared at a funnel cloud a few miles away, lightning shooting out of it like some movie special effect.

We had seen later on TV that one community had lost several houses and a couple of businesses, and three people had been killed.

Now water pummeled us, and Ashley and I ran. The drops turned harder. We ran to our old house and stood under the back eave.

I had taken a picture of Dad and Mom near the swings a few days before he died. It was with a really bad digital camera with about one pixel for your nose and one for the eyes, but it captured Dad's spirit. Mom was leaning against a pole, and Dad had an arm around her. He had that happy-go-lucky smile, and he looked at peace, like there wasn't one thing he wanted more than to be with his family.

Mom, on the other hand, didn't look happy. It could have been that the roses didn't do well that year or that Dylan was a handful as a baby, I guess, but Dad's smile looked even bigger because of the pain on Mom's face. That was before she became a Christian, so that probably had something to do with it.

Funny how a picture like that captures a moment, and just a few days later everything changes. I've seen pictures of soldiers right before they go out on a mission, smiling, eating together, and the next day their bodies are shipped back for a memorial service.

The fresh smell of rain washed over Ashley and me. You don't get this earthy kind of rain in Colorado, and it felt good. When it rains in Illinois, worms crawl out of their holes, looking for dry ground. They'll be all over the sidewalk, and you have to watch your step. I think the worms in Colorado go to Chicago for vacation.

It grew dark, kind of the way the whole trip had felt with the missing uncle and the panicky bride. Clouds that looked miles wide blew over.

Ashley shook every time lightning flashed. Then the thunder came, and it was Scared Central for both of us.

It started to hail, and just when the wind changed and started blowing some our way, the back door opened and the woman invited us in. She acted like she'd known us our whole lives, and I could tell she really liked Ashley.

I got the house tour. Every room reminded me of my dad, especially my old bedroom—even though it was pink. I closed my eyes and could almost hear him telling us a story or saying good night.

I was glad when it was time to go. All those memories can cloud your judgment, and we had a mystery to solve.

CHAPTER 57

✖ Ashley ✖

Carolyn asked if her dad would take us to a movie after dinner. Peggy was over. It was supposed to be the night of her rehearsal dinner, but of course it felt more like a funeral.

I could tell Peggy wasn't pretending. She cried, stared at the phone, grabbed more tissues, and cried some more.

We all waited for the phone to ring with any news—good or bad, it didn't matter. *Somebody call!* The longer we waited, the worse the tension got.

The only call came from Dustin, the camera operator at the commercial shoot. Mr. Hamilton told his wife that Dustin had heard about Larry and wanted to know if he could do anything.

"How sweet."

Mr. and Mrs. Hamilton decided a movie was a good idea, and Peggy actually looked relieved that we were leaving, which I could understand. When you're having a hard time, you want to be with friends, but not necessarily four teenagers. Carolyn went to tell Tim, and he came downstairs in an outfit that made him look more like a street person than an eighth grader.

Mr. Hamilton dropped us off, and as soon as we settled in, I noticed Tim wasn't with us.

After a few minutes, Bryce said, "I'll find him."

Bryce

I went all the way to the other end of the theater, looking everywhere, but there was no sign of Tim. I was heading back when I thought I saw Tim's jacket in the parking lot. I went to the head usher and explained that I needed to go outside.

"You'll have to pay to get back in."

I didn't want to do that, but I had to see who Tim was with. I walked to the front window, and suddenly there was Tim, waving at me. He pointed to the far end of the theater and headed that way.

I ran down the hall, wondering what he wanted. My stomach

tied in knots when I heard banging on the door. When I opened it, Tim and six others surged in.

"Hey, you can't—"

Tim waved. "Thanks, Timberline. Perfect timing."

They ducked into the first theater and left me standing there.

CHAPTER 59

✖ Ashley ✖

The previews hadn't begun, so I turned to Carolyn and whispered, "Your family really looks like it's struggling."

Carolyn frowned. "What do you mean?"

"It just seems like you guys are going in 20 different directions. Your dad's into work, your mom is in her own world, Tim is into I'm not sure what, and you—"

"We can't all be perfect like your family," Carolyn said.

That stung. "I'm not saying we're perfect. We've had a lot of problems. My stepsister is a pain—squared. My little brother gets on my nerves. And having my dad die messed us all up. What I'm saying is—"

"Why do you always play the dead-dad card? It's like we're all supposed to stop our lives when you say that."

My heart was beating as fast as a hummingbird's wings. Now I remembered why Carolyn and I hadn't kept in touch. If you brought up anything deeper than the latest fashions, she turned on you.

Instead of reacting like I wanted to, I took a deep breath. It's good when you're mad at someone to try to settle down and figure out what's really going on.

The trailers started and the lights dimmed.

"After your dad died things changed between us," Carolyn said. "And when you moved to Colorado, it felt like you were a million miles away. It was hard to tell you stuff, plus then you got really religious. We grew apart."

"Then why did you ask me to come? It couldn't have been just for the commercial."

"I missed our talks. I missed you. I thought maybe we'd get back what we used to have."

"When Mom became a Christian, I thought it was only a phase. Dad had been really into church and everything, and I went to make him happy."

"Do we have to talk about this?"

"You brought it up. Hear me out. Somewhere between the move to Colorado and Mom finding Sam and then church, God became real to me. Maybe it was all the change and the hurt, I don't know. Before then, God seemed to be all about rules or someone who wanted to kill your fun. But when I finally understood God actually cared about me, cared even more than my real dad could, it let me know he wanted to know me, not to just make me a good little girl who didn't do bad stuff."

"So?" Carolyn said.

"I'm trying to explain. You're right—I have changed. But there's more to it than us growing apart."

Carolyn sat back and folded her arms.

CHAPTER 60

🌚 *Bryce* 🌚

Tim and his friends had slipped into an R-rated movie. An usher in a red vest came by with a broom and a scooping tool. He nodded at me, and I imagined him going back to his boss and saying I was trying to sneak in, so I walked into the men's room.

My goal wasn't to see the movie but to find out more about Tim. I walked straight from the bathroom into the theater, turned left, and walked up a ramp. I waited until the screen was dark, then slipped into the first seat of the first row. It was a small theater so it didn't take me long to pinpoint Tim and his friends. They laughed and talked like a construction crew.

People were already turning around, sighing, and shaking their heads. I figured it wouldn't be long before some manager came and ran Tim and his friends out.

I hurried to the top of the stairs and sat on the other side. I stole a glance at them as they laughed. It was clear they hadn't seen me.

I moved a little closer, slid down in the seat, and listened.

"Got the stuff for tomorrow night?" one of them said.

"Yeah, already stashed," another said. "We're okay as long as pip-squeak here gets us in."

"I'll get you in," Tim said. "My dad has a key."

"Shh!" someone in front of them said.

"You shut up!" one of the guys said. Then they all laughed like it was the funniest thing in the history of the world.

A man stood and stomped down the stairs.

"What are they gonna do, kick us out?" Tim said. "It's not like we paid."

That brought another round of laughter.

I'd heard enough. I was glad to get out before the manager came.

CHAPTER 61

❈ Ashley ❈

I could tell Carolyn didn't want to talk because she just stared at the screen, though I knew she could see I was turned toward her. I finally gave up.

Bryce returned with a weird look. "Tim's plans for tomorrow night include some rough people," he whispered.

"How do you know?"

"I let them in the back door."

Tim and his friends piled into our theater, and Bryce shook his head. As far as I could tell, Tim didn't see us. They moved past and took the back row. There were two guys in jackets, then a couple hanging on to each other like they had superglue on their hands. The girl had bright blonde hair with touches of color. Two more guys followed, pushing each other into chairs.

I cringed when they started laughing and throwing popcorn. A cute kid came on the screen, and they hollered that his face looked like a pumpkin. The girl giggled at everything.

Loud as they were, no one seemed to mind until an older man with gray hair moved to the aisle. He had a little paunch, but other than that he looked pretty fit.

"What do *you* want, old man?" one of the guys said.

The man set his jaw.

"Come on, fatso," another said. "Think you can run us out?"

The man walked down the stairs and into the lobby.

People whispered and glared at the back row. You could feel the tension when someone called out, "Shut up back there!"

"Make us!"

Carolyn buried her head in her hands.

"You want to go?" I said.

She nodded and we stood. Bryce followed, and when we got to the door the older man was leading the manager inside.

"Is this them?" the manager said.

The man squinted and shook his head.

CHAPTER 62

☺ *Bryce* ☺

We moseyed outside, and through the front window I saw the theater manager leading Tim and the others out. Those characters looked even worse than when they were in the darkened theater. I figured they would probably be voted most likely to be incarcerated in the school yearbook.

"Does your dad have a key to any place near here?" I asked Carolyn.

She and Ashley looked at me like I'd just stepped out of a spaceship. "He carries lots of keys, why?"

"For what?" I said.

"His office, our house, Uncle Larry's place, the cabin by the lake, his cars—"

"What cabin?" I said.

"Just a shack, really. He bought it a few years ago to fix up."

"Where is it?"

She pointed. "That direction. We could probably walk from here, but it's in the middle of a preserve. Lots of woods around it. It feels like you're a million miles from civilization, even though it's really close."

"Let's check it out."

Ashley squinted at me. "What's all this about?"

I didn't want to tell either of them what I'd heard, so I pulled my tough-guy act. "You scared? It's just an old cabin. Plus, we've got time. Tim won't want us calling your dad too soon, or he'll find out Tim was kicked out of the theater. Come on."

I gave Ashley a smile, which meant *Don't mess this up, twin sister.*

She rolled her eyes.

CHAPTER 63

❀ Ashley ❀

Bryce stopped at a gas station and bought a flashlight and batteries. I was surprised how much the flashlight helped as Carolyn led us through a subdivision, then a little park.

She stopped next to a baseball field and pointed at a fence. "That's the edge of the preserve and the best way to get in."

The fence was about 12 feet high with three strands of barbed wire at the top. It bore a huge No Trespassing sign.

"It's okay," Carolyn said. "My dad owns the cabin, so the company said we can go through." She pulled a shrub away, revealing a hole in the fence.

We crawled through and found a path that led through the trees. The whole thing reminded me of the scene in *To Kill a Mockingbird* when Jem walks with Scout (who is dressed as a ham) through a dark, scary field.

Bryce walked ahead of us, shining the flashlight on the path. The moon lay behind clouds, but elsewhere I could see stars.

We'd been walking about 10 minutes when Carolyn motioned to a shiny area. "That's the lake. Cabin's on the other side."

I noticed a weird yellow glow in the middle of the lake. The water rippled and ducks swam by. Bryce turned off his flashlight.

"What?" Carolyn said.

"There's a light on inside the cabin."

CHAPTER 64

☺ *Bryce* ☺

"Could your dad be in there?" I said.

Carolyn craned her neck. "You have to park about 50 yards from the cabin. I don't see anyone parked there."

When the hair on the back of my neck stands on end, that's a signal I'm on to something. We continued around the lake, keeping an eye on the cabin. As we got closer, someone's silhouette passed a window.

The moon came out from behind a cloud, revealing a small porch that looked like it might fall through if you stepped on it. I was surprised, because Mr. Hamilton was used to nice things.

"Dad wanted to keep it in its original condition," Carolyn said. "They've done work on the inside, but they've left the outside alone."

"Ever come out here as a family?" Ashley whispered.

"Tim and I came last winter to skate. It gets so cold in there you can see your breath. No electricity, no refrigerator . . ."

"Then where's the light coming from?" Ashley said.

"Good question," she said.

When my cell phone rang, the light inside the cabin went out.

"Bryce, this is Carolyn's dad. What happened?"

"What do you mean, sir?" I whispered, watching the cabin.

"Tim called—said there was a problem. I'm at the theater now. Where are you?"

I hesitated. "At your cabin."

"What!?" He sounded like I had launched a nuclear missile at Ridgefield. "You come back here this instant!"

"Sir, there's a light on in the cabin . . . at least there was. Is someone staying here?"

He sighed. "Give the phone to Carolyn."

She said a lot of I'm-sorry-Dads and we-didn't-mean-tos, and she promised we'd come right back to the theater.

"I'm not leaving until we see who's in there," I said.

She grabbed the flashlight. "Then find your own way back. My dad said to come *now*."

"Aren't you curious?" Ashley said.

I heard a door creak open, then close. I snatched the flashlight from Carolyn and ran toward the cabin. I heard footsteps in the dry leaves and pointed the light that direction, but whoever it was had run over a little ridge and was out of sight.

I went to the cabin door and turned the knob. There was a kerosene smell inside and a lantern on the table. It was still hot. A sleep-ing bag lay on a couch in the corner, and canned food sat on the counter. A loaf of bread lay unopened, and the stale date showed it had been bought recently.

"Whoever was here must have had a key," Ashley said. "The windows aren't broken, and the lock is fine."

I wanted to go through the cabin inch by inch.

But Carolyn looked annoyed. "Listen, I have to go back. My dad will be really ticked."

CHAPTER 65

❀ Ashley ❀

Back at the theater parking lot Tim sat in the front seat of their SUV scowling. His weird-looking friends were nowhere in sight, and I wondered what he'd told his dad.

"What were you thinking, Carolyn, taking them to the cabin?" Mr. Hamilton said.

"It was my idea," Bryce said. "And, sir, there's someone—"

"I don't appreciate your going off without my permission, and I don't think your parents would either." He drove through the parking lot.

"Mr. Hamilton," I said, "someone was in your cabin. The light was on, and then it went out, and we found food inside."

He stopped the car. "Did you see anyone?"

"Whoever it was ran out."

"We've had homeless people there in the past," Carolyn said.

"Yeah, probably some guy down on his luck," Mr. Hamilton said. "I'll call the police when we get home."

"Don't you want to take a look?" I said. "Lock the door so they can't get back in?"

"That is, unless you know who's there," Bryce said.

Mr. Hamilton glared in the rearview mirror. "Of course I don't know who it is! Fine, we'll lock it up."

"Take me home first," Tim said.

Mr. Hamilton said, "If you have to get back, I'll take you."

I couldn't believe it. We drove all the way to their house and let Tim out. Mr. Hamilton said he would check the cabin alone, but we pleaded with him to let us come along. He finally agreed but went inside briefly before we left. Tim must have gone upstairs because we heard a door slam up there from the driveway. Mrs. Hamilton's car was gone.

Mr. Hamilton drove back to the preserve, and we finally came to the parking spot that overlooked the cabin. The headlights cast an eerie shadow on the place.

Bryce, Carolyn, and I followed Mr. Hamilton down the hill. He tried the doorknob but now had to use the key to get in. That kerosene smell was still there, but the food had been cleared and the sleeping bag was gone.

Bryce gave me a look. "Who else has a key to this place?"

Mr. Hamilton rubbed his chin. "The company has a key in case of an emergency, and I keep a couple of spares at home."

"Any of those missing?" Bryce said.

Mr. Hamilton shrugged. "I'll look."

"Someone could have made a copy," Carolyn said.

"True," her father said. "Anyone who's been here since we bought it could have." He glanced around. "Whoever it was didn't take anything, so it's probably not worth bothering the police."

Bryce looked outside for footprints or other clues but didn't find anything.

I tried looking inside, but all we had was one flashlight.

PART 5

CHAPTER 66

SATURDAY

☺ *Bryce* ☺

I didn't sleep well on the couch. I'd get comfortable, then get too hot and go turn on the overhead fan, then get too cold, turn it off, and try to get comfortable again. Finally I just lay there mulling over the mystery of the cabin.

That Tim had wanted to go home could have been a trick to give his friends time to get out. But Mr. Hamilton not calling the police or even seeming that worried about the cabin made me more suspicious of him.

Breakfast was a somber affair. Peggy showed up but barely ate. She pushed some kind of strawberry-flavored health cereal around her bowl until it turned to mush. Who could blame her? Today was supposed to be her wedding day, and that wasn't going to happen.

"Did you check those keys?" I asked Mr. Hamilton.

He snapped his fingers. "Forgot." He went into the pantry and moved something around in a drawer, then came back with a worried look. "One is missing."

Mrs. Hamilton didn't know anything and wondered why he was worried about a key at a time like this. The whole thing made me suspicious that Mr. Hamilton had done something with it himself.

Tim wasn't up yet, and his mom said he slept in on Saturdays. I envied him because I have chores every Saturday and couldn't imagine getting up whenever I wanted.

I was downstairs with Ashley watching SportsCenter and kicking around ideas when we heard the doorbell. I muted the TV, and we heard footsteps going toward the door, the door opening, a squeal, and a cry. Then a thump.

We raced upstairs.

CHAPTER 67

✖ Ashley ✖

I've seen enough of those war movies where the chaplain visits the wife or mother of a dead soldier to imagine Peggy getting bad news from the police and fainting.

Sure enough, we found Peggy on the living-room floor with Mrs. Hamilton waving a dish towel over her. Mr. Hamilton stood at the door with a deliveryman who was holding a huge white box that said *Wedding Cake Creations.*

"Just put it in the kitchen," Mr. Hamilton said.

Bryce and I decided to visit Larry's office again.

"Maybe Tucker is the one with the key to the cabin," he said.

"What would he be doing there?"

Bryce shrugged. "Maybe the police are on to him. Let's see if we can get into his office and snoop around."

We signed in and asked the security guard whether Mr. Brooks was upstairs.

"He signed in at 9:30, but I wouldn't know if he's still there."

All the offices were dark except Tucker's. We moved slowly, but as we drew close we heard no movement or tapping of the keyboard. Finally we peeked in. His desk was a mess of used coffee mugs and cups, napkins and paper, even a wrapper for an iced breakfast roll that looked a thousand years old.

Suddenly the chair turned around and Tucker stared at us, a cell phone to his ear. His eyes were glassy and red.

"Sorry," Bryce said, stepping back.

Tucker clicked his cell phone shut. "The police found a body this morning. They think it might be Larry's."

CHAPTER 68

◑ *Bryce* ◑

Ashley and I sprinted back to the Hamiltons' house
and found a police car and a gaggle of neighbors in front. We heard
crying inside, so we waited on the porch.

An officer came out and tipped his hat as he got into his car.

Finally Carolyn came out.

"Is it Larry?" Ashley said, a hand over her mouth.

Carolyn shook her head. "They found someone, but it wasn't
him."

Tucker's shock and fear had seemed genuine. That didn't rule him out, of course. His could have been tears of guilt, but it made me want to consider other suspects.

Time was running out, though. We had only one more day to crack the case, and I wanted to follow Tim when he went to meet his friends.

Carolyn told the neighbors, and the crowd dispersed. A car that I didn't recognize pulled up.

Dustin, the camera guy, emerged with something in his hand. "Carolyn home?"

Ashley pointed.

"Ah, well, I'm sorry to bother the family at such a difficult time, but I heard something on the news about Mr. Hamilton's brother. That they found a body?"

Ashley told him what we'd heard, and relief swept over his face. "Um, I knew you were leaving town, so I thought I'd give you a copy of the commercial. You two did well. I was pleased."

"I just hope we didn't make fools of ourselves," Ashley said.

Carolyn escorted Dustin inside to talk with her father.

I snagged the DVD from Ashley. "Come on—let's go watch."

"Not on your life," she said. "This is no time to watch a furniture commercial."

"A little tiger and kangaroo might cheer them up," I said.

"It was a lion and a zebra," she said, grabbing the DVD.

I turned and noticed that Dustin's car was a stick shift, one of those classic Mustangs. I drooled. Just what I want when I'm old enough.

"What are you doing?" Ashley said as I climbed in.

"Just want to see what it feels like." I put a hand on the steering wheel and gripped the gearshift. I imagined myself heading toward I-25, free as a bird, unshackled from parents and sisters and little brothers. I'd have my own job. Meet friends at the movies. Go out to dinner.

What I didn't imagine was what I saw on the passenger seat.

CHAPTER 69

❀ Ashley ❀

Bryce's face turned white as a sheet, like he'd spilled chocolate syrup all over Dustin's upholstery. I leaned in and looked at what he was pointing at—an unzipped green bag. It was full of cash. Lots of it.

Bryce opened it with a finger. "It's 50s and 20s . . . and 100s."

"Where would he get all that? And why would he carry it around?"

"Can I help you?" Dustin said.

I nearly jumped over the car. I could tell he wanted to yell at us, because the veins in his neck stuck out.

Bryce jumped out and said, "I've been looking at old Mustangs like this one. Cool car. Did you learn on a stick?"

"Did I what?"

"When you learned to drive, did you start with a stick shift or an automatic, because I think if you start with a stick you can switch to an automatic easier than the other way around."

"I learned on an automatic. Now what were you doing—?"

"I guess it could work either way," Bryce said. "I just think if you start with a stick you can drive anything."

Dustin slid in and slammed the door. He closed the money bag, fired up the engine, and pulled away.

CHAPTER 70

☺ *Bryce* ☺

Mr. Hamilton said the body the police found turned out
to be that of a guy who'd fallen overboard on a boat outing. I was
glad it wasn't Larry, of course, but someone else's family would be
having a funeral soon.

I wanted to get back to Colorado, but I also wanted to stay until
Larry was found. We had only one more day.

Ashley and I put our heads together in Carolyn's room, pulling
Post-it notes and writing clues.

"What about Dustin?" Ashley said.

"Having a lot of cash doesn't make you guilty of anything, but it does raise questions."

We threw out ideas, trying to think of every angle. We even wondered if Carolyn or Tim could be involved.

When Carolyn came back upstairs, I stashed the notes and left Ashley and her alone. I checked my watch and wondered how long it would be until Tim met his friends.

CHAPTER 71

✖ Ashley ✖

"Do you ever wonder what your life would be like if your dad hadn't died?" Carolyn said.

"All the time. We'd probably still be living here. You and I would still be best friends. On the other hand, I'm not sure my mom would be a Christian, and we'd never have met all the people we've met the last few years."

I told her about Boo Heckler, the school bully, and what I'd learned about his past. Then I described Sam and Leigh and what our house was like in Colorado. Suddenly I was homesick.

"Do you ever wonder if the whole God thing is real or if we're making all that up?" Carolyn said.

Sometimes people need to answer their own questions, so I just looked at her with my "listening eyes."

"The stuff I said about you, you know, that your life is all pretty and nice and you go to church and everything. I think I'm jealous because things have fallen apart here."

"You mean with Tim?"

"Not just Tim." She sighed and puffed her cheeks out. "I used to think if you memorized verses, listened to the Christian radio station, hummed hymns, and watched Christian music videos, everything would turn out right."

"But all that doesn't guarantee smooth sailing," I said.

"Right. I mean, I thought everything was fine, but Tim started hanging with the wrong crowd, Mom and Dad had some problems, and now this thing with Uncle Larry. He's one of the nicest people in our whole church. . . ." She looked up. "Ashley, I don't even know if I believe in God anymore."

CHAPTER 72

○ *Bryce* ○

Tim's music started at about three o'clock in the afternoon, and I guessed that's when he finally got up. He must have been planning a big night out.

I borrowed Tim's bike, which his mother said he hadn't used in a year. I rode by the high school and saw people cleaning up from the football game the night before. I kept turning the information about Larry over in my head—things people had said, all the information I had.

Then I thought about Mrs. Hamilton's keys, and I slammed my

brakes so hard I almost went over the handlebars. How could I have missed it?

I had stopped in front of Tina Workman's house. You weren't supposed to like girls when you were in grade school, but she'd had the prettiest eyes, the softest hair, a cute nose, and she'd invited me to her birthday party in third grade. That's the one where I ate too much cake and pizza, then played freeze tag in the backyard until . . .

"Bryce?"

I was so deep in thought that I hadn't seen her at the door. The only girl who had ever kissed me. It wasn't actually a kiss—it was more a dare from her friends. I had been standing by the merry-go-round, and she'd ambushed me. I turned red and everybody laughed.

"That *is* you, Bryce! I didn't know you were back."

She was even prettier than I remembered, and her hair was just as silky smooth.

I wanted to say something suave, but all that came out was, "Hey, Tina."

She approached, smiling, and I saw her braces. Even they looked cute on her. "I don't think I've seen you since you barfed on our doghouse."

Funny how such a cute girl can bring up such a terrible moment, and it doesn't even bother me. "Yeah, that was a great party, wasn't it?"

She studied me. "Have you moved back?"

"No, just visiting."

"That's a shame. I'm sorry about your dad."

"Yeah."

"Your mom okay?"

I nodded. "Well, I gotta go."

"So soon?"

"There's something I have to do."

She sighed. "Call me sometime. E-mail me or something."

"Yeah, I will."

CHAPTER 73

❀ Ashley ❀

Bryce was out of breath when he got back. As he explained his theory about Larry, I thought he was joking, but the more he talked, the less I argued. He told me how to find out if he was right.

"Isn't that like lying?" I said.

"In a way, I guess. Any better ideas?"

It wasn't easy following his hunch and working this without Carolyn, but Bryce said it was for the best. I wanted to tell him about the talk I had with her. I hadn't convinced her of anything, but I did tell her that struggling with her faith proved she had some and to not give up on God just because things were getting tough.

Bryce and I secretly scrounged up a couple of old walkie-talkies in the garage, and Bryce took off on the bike.

I found Mrs. Hamilton in the kitchen on the phone. I searched the refrigerator like I was digging for a golden nugget.

When she finally hung up, I sat and said, "Any news?"

She shook her head.

I stood as if to leave. "Well, it shouldn't be too much longer if Bryce is right."

"Has he heard something?"

I nodded. "We're interested in mysteries. There were these people who wanted to steal alpacas from a farm near—"

"What about your brother? What did he find out?"

"He said he'd uncovered information about Larry and was going to find him."

"Really? Did he say where he was going?"

I shook my head.

"How long has he been gone?"

"A few minutes."

She looked out the window.

I pointed toward the end of the street. "He went that way."

Mrs. Hamilton reacted just like Bryce said she would. She grabbed her keys and ran to the garage.

"Want me to go with you?" I yelled.

"I'm fine," she called. "Be right back."

CHAPTER 74

☺ *Bryce* ☺

It was the same tactic I'd used with Leigh a couple of years before. I'd overheard her telling a friend she'd buried some old love letters behind our house. I tried to find them. She finally asked what I was looking for, and I told her.

She shook her head. "You'll never find them."

"We'll see," I said.

I came running through the house the next day with a faded letter I'd found in one of Sam's old stashes. I laughed and said, "Told you I'd find them" and ran to my room.

Leigh pounded on my door, but I didn't care how much she

huffed and puffed. As soon as she went downstairs, I got out the bin-
oculars and watched her walk behind the barn and into the field.
She got about halfway to the red rocks and started digging. Not long
after that I saw a thin trail of smoke. She burned the letters, and I
never got to read them, but my plan had worked—sort of.

"Mrs. Hamilton's coming your way," Ashley's voice squawked
on the walkie-talkie. "You were right—she ran right to the car as
soon as I told her."

"10-4," I said. I've always wanted to say that.

I was on the other side of the Dairy Queen when Mrs. Hamilton
pulled to the stoplight. "She's turning left toward the theaters," I
said. "I'll never be able to keep up."

"At least we know which direction she's going."

"10-4," I said. Twice in one day. Pretty cool. "I'm headed your
way."

I pedaled as fast as I could and was out of breath when I reached
the Hamiltons'. We asked Carolyn if there were any other cabins or
empty houses near the theaters.

She shook her head. "Just the one at the lake. Why?"

"I think your uncle is okay," I said.

"How do you know?"

"I think he's hiding, but I have no idea why."

CHAPTER 75

✖ Ashley ✖

When Mrs. Hamilton returned she seemed calmer. "Is your brother here?"

I nodded. "But he didn't find Larry. Guess it was a bad hunch."

She talked with Bryce and insisted he tell her what he knew. Bryce said something about seeing clues at the cabin.

"I'm following Tim tonight," Bryce said when we were alone. "Stick with Mrs. Hamilton."

"How am I supposed to do that?"

"Do whatever you have to. Just stay with her."

"You think she'll go out tonight?"

"I'm positive."

Could Bryce be right? Why would Mrs. Hamilton keep such a secret from the rest of the family and especially from Peggy?

With all the activity over the past few days, I found myself exhausted and lay on Carolyn's bed. Soon I fell asleep and dreamed about a Bengal tiger attacking a kangaroo with a wooden spoon covered with peanut butter. It was not your normal vacation dream, and I was glad when Carolyn woke me for dinner. We had brat-wurst and burgers cooked on the grill by Mr. Hamilton. The smoky smell and sizzling meat brought back memories of my own dad doing the same thing.

Carolyn, Bryce, and I played croquet, but it wasn't like an ordinary cookout with people laughing and playing volleyball. Naturally, everyone seemed tense and subdued.

Bryce kept looking up at Tim's window. I kept an eye on Mrs. Hamilton, wondering when and if she might go out. It was the longest cookout of my life.

As soon as it started getting dark, I told everyone I was tired and went to Carolyn's room, where I stretched out in a sleeping bag on the floor. I sat up and studied how my body looked in the bag, then got up and stuffed a bunch of my clothes inside and zipped it up. I grabbed an old blanket from Carolyn's closet and snuck into the garage. I lay on the floor behind the front seat of Mrs. Hamilton's car and tried to get comfortable.

Now all I had to do was wait. And wait. And wait.

CHAPTER 76

☻ *Bryce* ☻

I stayed alert for any movement from Tim's room.
At about 10 I moved onto the back patio. There was that crisp feeling of fall you get in Illinois. Colorado summers run right into winter, but here things change gradually, which I guess is why the leaves looked so bright and colorful. Not in the dark, but you know what I mean.

The light in Tim's room was still on, and I wrapped a blanket around me, even though I had my jean jacket on. Just after 11 his light went out. I stashed my stuff inside and listened at the stairs.

Nothing.

Back outside I noticed Tim's window was open. Latticework with lots of ivy growing on it ran up the side of the house. Tim stepped onto the lattice and started down. I slipped behind some bushes and waited. I had a sinking feeling his friends would pick him up and leave me in the dust, so I was relieved when he grabbed his skateboard and hurried off down the street.

I followed, careful to be quiet. I told Ashley to turn her walkie-talkie low, just in case either of us got in trouble. Mine was off now and heavy in my pocket.

When Tim got to the park near our old house, his skateboard *clack-clack*ed over the cracks in the concrete. I ran in the field to keep up, peeking over the ridge that rose above the sidewalk. Tim passed the library and picked up speed. He was heading in the opposite direction from the cabin.

Finally Tim jumped off his skateboard, picked it up, crossed the street, then continued down a lane. I realized where he was going when I saw familiar houses. He didn't hesitate, didn't look back. When he reached Larry's house, seven people got out of a car parked across the street. They were the same ones who'd been with him at the theater, plus one more girl. She giggled as they walked up the steps to Larry's house.

"Got the key?" the tallest one said.

Tim held it up and unlocked the front door. He held it open while everyone went in, then looked around behind him before entering.

CHAPTER 77

❀ Ashley ❀

The hump in the middle of the floor of the backseat made me
so uncomfortable I had to move to the seat. I covered up and listened for anyone, checking the walkie-talkie frequently for any message from Bryce.

The clock on the radio glowed green. At 11:27, a shaft of light lit
the garage. The garage door opened, and I slid onto the floor, pulling
the blanket over me.

Someone got in the car, started it, and backed up. I heard the garage door closing as we pulled away. Streetlights flashed as we
picked up speed. We were heading north, then west, but after a few

turns, I couldn't figure out where we were. The radio clicked onto a Christian station, and the announcer had a deep voice. It sounded like the music was aimed at putting people to sleep.

The driver hummed, and for the first time I was sure it was Mrs. Hamilton. Then the radio clicked off, and she punched numbers on a phone.

"I'm almost there," she said. "Do you have the discs? . . . I'll look for you in the parking lot in two minutes."

My heart felt like it was going to hop out of my chest and do a little dance on the backseat, but I took deep breaths and calmed myself. We went around a big curve, then over a big bump, and slowed. I wanted to sit up and see where we were, but of course I couldn't.

More punching of numbers. "I'm almost at the rendezvous. You still at the cabin? . . . Where? . . . How'd you get over there? Someone will see you."

The car stopped and Mrs. Hamilton hung up, then grabbed something from the passenger seat. She stepped out and left the door open, and I heard her walk away from the car.

"You have the money?" a man said. His voice sounded familiar.

"The whole $5,000," Mrs. Hamilton said, her voice shaky.

"I made it clear to Larry that the cost doubled if he waited," the man said, his voice strained. "It's 10 grand, not 5."

"But—"

"He gives me the full amount or I turn the discs over to the media and tell the authorities."

"I don't think he can get that kind of money—"

"I know he has it. Tell him to get it to me tonight. I'll give him two hours."

Bryce

I knelt across the street from Larry's as lights came on throughout the house. A dog barked behind me, and I ran to a row of shrubs near Larry's front steps. From there I moved to the side of the house, shrouded in darkness. I let my eyes adjust, stepping over a garden hose.

A window at ground level let me see inside the basement. Tall Guy bounded down the stairs with Tim right behind, like a tail-wagging puppy. Tim pointed at a cabinet in the corner. Tall Guy opened it and grabbed several bottles, put them under his arms, and carried them upstairs.

I wondered if it was alcohol and whether Tim had stashed it there.

Music blared and made the windows shake. I found a cinder block and tipped it up so I could stand on it. The others upstairs were dancing—sort of like chickens with bad shoes—and raiding the refrigerator. Basically, they were trashing the house.

My walkie-talkie squawked, but I could barely hear Ashley because she was whispering. She was back at the Hamiltons' house in the backseat of Mrs. Hamilton's car. Ashley told me I had been right, that Mrs. Hamilton had met some guy in a parking lot, then called Larry about paying for something. For the first time we knew for sure he was alive.

"Good work," I said. "Did it sound like Larry was nearby?"

"He's not at the cabin—that's all I know. I just can't believe she's known about this all along. What do you think she's up to?"

"Haven't figured it out, but—"

Someone came to the window and looked outside.

I ducked behind a bush and clicked off the walkie-talkie. My watch light glowed. It was almost midnight.

The music stopped and the window opened. Tall Guy stuck his head out, his hair hanging like Rapunzel's.

"What is it?" one of the girls said.

"Thought I saw someone."

"You're paranoid," Tim said, laughing, "and you know why."

Tall Guy moved away from the window. "Shut up!" he said, gritting his teeth. "You don't talk about anything we've done. Who do you think you are?"

Several others berated Tim, yelling at him and punching him.

He tried not to cry, but I could tell by the whine in his voice that he was hurting. "I didn't mean anything by it! Come on—I let you guys in like I said I would. You said I'd be a member."

"Right, but you have to prove yourself," Tall Guy said.

"What do you call getting the booze and trashing that trophy case?"

"A good start."

"Okay, what else?"

"What do you think, Bones?"

Bones was skinny with long fingers. "Burn it," he said finally.

"Great idea," Tall Guy said.

"What do you mean?" Tim said. "Burn what?"

"The house," Tall Guy said. "Burn it to the ground. It's perfect."

"That's a bad idea," Tim said. "This is my uncle's place and—"

"You want to be part of us?"

"Well, yeah—"

"Then burn it."

"I don't know, guys. . . ."

Tall Guy said, "There're matches in the kitchen. Bones, get the gas can out of the car."

I had to think fast.

PART 6

CHAPTER 79

SUNDAY

✖ Ashley ✖

Mrs. Hamilton had parked on the street outside her house and walked in through the garage. I tried Bryce again, but he was out of range or had turned off his walkie-talkie.

Why would he do that?

My back felt like I had been sleeping on one of those nail mattresses on the amazing-things shows where people hang from the Eiffel Tower by their teeth or pull a 757 with their eyebrows. But I didn't want to leave the car if Mrs. Hamilton was coming back.

I sat up and noticed that all the lights in the house were off and

Mrs. Hamilton had shut the garage. If she locked the inside door I wasn't getting back inside. I lay on the backseat and covered up, feeling a chill as the night settled like a blanket of dew.

I tried Bryce again on the walkie-talkie.

Nothing.

CHAPTER 80

☺ *Bryce* ☺

Bones grabbed the gas can from the car and walked like he was on stilts—that's how skinny his legs were. He was back in the house before I'd even come up with a plan.

I raced to the back of the house and crept up the steps. Through a window I saw Bones sloshing gas on the floor, the rest standing around like they were watching a pro-wrestling match.

I banged on the door three times—with authority.

The music stopped. Girls screamed. Bones said, "Who's that?"

I jumped down the steps, rushed to the side window, and held up my walkie-talkie, turning it on and off several times so it squawked like a police radio.

Tall Guy ran to the front door. "Everybody in the car! Except you, Tim. Stay here and light it."

"I-I-I . . ."

"We don't see a burning building here, you're not one of us. Got it?"

The front door flew open, and they ran across the street to their car.

I went to the front and entered.

Tim's mouth dropped open. "What're you doin' here?"

"That was me at the back door."

"How did you know . . . ?"

"Come on," I said. "Get some rags and let's wipe the gas from the hardwood floor before it ruins it."

The place smelled like a gas station, but once we sopped up all the fuel, it didn't look so bad. We turned off the lights and sat in the dark, neither saying anything for a long time.

"I knew you didn't want to start any fire," I said finally.

"Yeah, thanks." He ran a hand through his hair. "Guess I'm lucky you followed me. Why did you?"

"Everybody changes as they grow up, but this isn't you, Tim. Why'd you want to get in with such losers?"

The whole story spilled. Tim had tried out for basketball in middle school and had been cut. Then the crowd he usually ran with didn't accept him anymore. He didn't fit in with the kids at church. They seemed so good, and he knew he wasn't.

"Then out of the blue my girlfriend says she wants to just be friends. I guess that pushed me over the edge. The rest of the summer I let my hair grow, found somebody who would put this in—"

he pointed to the nose ring—"and started dressing this way. Didn't take those guys long to notice me, and they let me hang with them."

"And they put you up to smashing the middle school trophy case?"

He nodded. "I'm not proud of it, but I didn't care if I got caught. But now . . . I don't want to destroy Uncle Larry's place. I figured he would be gone on his honeymoon, we'd party, and I'd clean up before he got back. Didn't expect him to disappear."

"I'm just glad you didn't torch the place before we got all his Cubs stuff out."

That made him chuckle. "When I heard you were coming with your sister, I figured you'd probably preach to me. I heard you and Ashley got religious."

"I don't know about *religious*," I said, "but I think God has something he wants me to do."

"Like what?"

A shadow passed the front window.

I put a finger to my lips as footsteps creaked on the front porch. The lock jiggled and the front door opened.

CHAPTER 81

❋ Ashley ❋

I jolted awake, scared to death, as someone tapped on the window.

"What are you doing out here?" Carolyn said.

"Couldn't sleep," I said, opening the door.

Carolyn got in. "What's up?"

"Something's bugging me. It has been ever since I got here, and I don't know how to—"

"Just say it. What's the problem?"

I traced my finger along a line in the blanket. "It's about you and guys. And God."

"There's nothing wrong with liking guys. And I go to church."

"I want to be your friend," I said. "And maybe I'm not doing a good job of explaining. But I'd like to tell you more about what God's done for me. If you'll listen."

"Now?"

The garage opened, and Mrs. Hamilton walked toward us.

Carolyn didn't seem to believe her mother was still up.

"Get on the floor," I whispered.

CHAPTER 82

☺ *Bryce* ☺

A man entered and went straight downstairs.

"Who was that?" I whispered.

"I think it was Uncle Larry," Tim said.

We tiptoed to the stairs as a light came on in the basement. We crept down and saw Larry throwing books off a shelf and moving a picture. Behind it was a safe with a combination lock, which he turned left and right a few times before it opened. Larry pulled out documents and envelopes until he got to the back of the safe.

Suddenly he turned and saw us, dropping a stack of money and grabbing his chest. "What are you doing here, Tim? And who's this?"

"An old friend. Where have you been, Uncle Larry?"

Larry stuffed everything but the money back in the safe. "You need to go home."

"You missed your own wedding," Tim said. "Peggy's been at our house crying enough to raise the Mississippi."

Larry headed for the stairs.

"It's got something to do with Dustin, doesn't it?" I said.

That stopped him.

"And Mrs. Hamilton is helping you."

"How do you know that?"

"One key on her key ring has a Cubs insignia, but she's a big Sox fan. Plus, there's a key to the cabin. She took you there."

He just stared at me.

I told him about our investigation and what Ashley had discovered. "Tell us what happened, sir."

Finally he sat on an old sofa. "I've been running from this for days, and you think I'm going to tell you?"

"We might be able to help," I said. "Why did you come for the money?"

"To pay off Dustin. He has some discs I need."

"What kind of discs?" Tim said.

"Video. Now you two get out of here before—"

"This has nothing to do with Tucker?" I said. "He was at the Cubs game Thursday in your seat."

"No, Tucker's not involved." Larry got a weird look on his face. "Do you smell gasoline? What are you doing here, anyway?"

I told him we'd run some bad characters out of his house, and Tim looked at me like he wanted to buy me a present. I pummeled Larry with questions.

He said he hadn't planned on disappearing but felt he had to.

"You've been staying at the cabin?"

He nodded. "Just until I could get my head together."

"Mom is in on this?" Tim said.

Larry held out a hand, like he was pleading. "She was only trying to help me, you understand? She was the only one I could go to."

"Go to with what?" Tim said.

Larry put his face in his hands. "Let's just say Dustin has some footage of me I don't want anyone to see. If I get it, I can go back to Peggy, apologize—"

"What kind of footage?" Tim said.

"I told you, I don't want to talk about it."

Tim shook his head. "Every TV station in Chicago has your picture. You can't show up now and expect everyone to hug you and not ask questions. Your friends and family deserve answers."

Larry shook his head. He sat back, clutched his stomach, and sighed. "I love Peggy, but the closer the wedding got, the more I felt the pressure. So I went down to the casinos on the river. Those people don't care if you're a church leader or a drunk—they just want your money. One trip turned into two. I thought it was just harmless fun, but then I found myself going back every day. It wasn't just the gambling. I started drinking alcohol too."

"I don't get it," Tim said. "Why would that make you hide?"

"This guy shot a video of me in the casinos. I'd had some drinks, laughed it up with the people around the table. Women around the table. Next thing I know there's a DVD in my box at work. I stick it in my computer and see the whole thing. The guy who shot it asked for money. That's when I went to your mother."

"Why not Dad?" Tim said.

"Trust me, your father couldn't have handled it. Your mom suggested I tell Peggy and talk to our pastor, but I couldn't. I begged her

to drive my car to the airport to make it look like I'd left town.
I thought the guy would leave me alone and I could get my head together."

"That was the day we got here," I said. "That's why Mrs. Hamilton couldn't pick us up. And the noise Ashley heard in the background was from O'Hare. Now the guy wants 10 thousand instead
of 5."

Larry nodded.

Tim said, "You know the verse that says 'the truth will set you
free'? If you tell people your problem and get help, you won't have
to pay this guy. Peggy will understand—she loves you. Everybody
cares about you. Anyway, how do you know if you pay him off that
he didn't keep a copy and could blackmail you the rest of your life?"

Larry's brow furrowed, as if Tim were speaking French.

"Plus," I said, "I think this Dustin character is doing the same
thing to other people." I told him of the newspaper listing of a wedding that Dustin had circled. "That wedding was called off too. This
guy needs to be stopped."

CHAPTER 83

✖ Ashley ✖

Mrs. Hamilton kept pulling tissues from a box on the dash, blowing her nose, and tossing them in the backseat.

She punched numbers on her phone. "It's me. Did you get the money? . . . What? . . . Yeah, I can arrange that, but, Larry . . . okay, I'll do it."

She dialed another number. "He wants you to come to his house. . . . He has the money, but he wants to do this face-to-face. . . . All right, 20 minutes."

As soon as Mrs. Hamilton hung up, my radio squawked. "Ashley, you still there?" Bryce said.

Mrs. Hamilton jerked around and gasped. Carolyn and I sat up. "What in the world . . . ?"

"I'm here, Bryce," I said. "Give me a minute."

I tried to explain, but it came out all wrong.

Finally Carolyn said I was trying to help. "You should let her talk to Bryce."

"Go ahead," Mrs. Hamilton said.

"Okay, Bryce, go," I said.

Bryce filled me in and said, "Wake Carolyn and get her digital recorder. Tim says she has one of those tiny things you can stick in a shirt pocket."

"I'll get it," Carolyn whispered, getting out of the car.

"Meet us at Larry's house as fast as you can," Bryce said.

CHAPTER 84

☺ *Bryce* ☺

Every few minutes Larry would have second thoughts, and we'd have to talk him out of giving Dustin the money.

"Hey," I said, "if *we* can handle your confession, Peggy can too."

"Yeah," Tim said, "you can't run anymore. Face this."

I glanced at Tim and believed he was talking to himself as much as to his uncle. He was going to have to face his new "friends" too.

When Mrs. Hamilton arrived, Larry hurried out and told her to park up the street. Carolyn hugged her uncle, and he said he couldn't wait to call Peggy.

Carolyn handed him the recorder. "What do you want this for?"

"There's no time to explain everything to the police," he said. "We have to get Dustin to admit what he's been doing."

Carolyn, Ashley, and Mrs. Hamilton hid in the dark house. Tim hid in some bushes up the street, and Larry sat on the porch. I stood in a dark corner of the porch behind a pole.

"Guess I royally messed up," Larry said.

"You did," I said. "But either we believe you can be forgiven or we don't."

"I know God will forgive me," he said. "It's everybody else."

The Mustang pulled up and stopped across the street. Dustin got out, carrying a couple of discs.

Larry stood and seemed to move with purpose, his chest out. He pushed the Record button inside his shirt pocket.

"You have the money?" Dustin said from the sidewalk.

Larry moved down the steps and stopped a few feet from him. "Did you destroy the masters?"

Dustin nodded and held up the discs. "These are the only two copies."

"Well, that's fine, but I don't think I'm interested. I'm done running."

"If the people at your church and your future wife see this—"

"Oh, they will. I'll show them. They may kick me out of the church. They might not want anything to do with me."

"So give me the money and it all goes away."

"Even if I destroy those, I'll still have to explain why I went away, missed my own wedding. I'll know the truth."

"I'll go to the media. This story is big enough that they'll pay for them."

"Doesn't it bother you to make a living hurting people? I'm not the first person you've tried this with, am I?"

"And you won't be the last. You'd be surprised what people are willing to pay to keep their secrets. And everybody has a secret."

"What do you do, find wedding announcements in the paper and follow the bride and groom until you find some dirt?"

"Believe me, it isn't that hard. A little research into people's lives, ask a few questions, and you find out a lot."

I signaled Ashley, and the faint tones of a telephone keypad sounded inside the house.

"Come on, Larry," Dustin said. "You don't want people seeing these. Give me the money and you can just say you got cold feet. Nobody has to know the truth."

Out of nowhere a black streak flew down the sidewalk.

Dustin looked up, but by the time he saw him, Tim had run past, grabbed the discs, and raced away.

Dustin toppled backward, then jumped up and ran after Tim. As quickly as he'd gone into the street, Tim changed direction and darted the other way, avoiding Dustin and tossing the discs my way. I caught one, and the other clattered on the porch.

I ran to the other side of the porch and grabbed the fallen disc just as Dustin reached me. I tossed them both to Larry. Dustin turned as a siren sounded in the distance.

"I'd pay for these now," Larry said, smirking. "They're not evidence against me anymore. They're evidence against *you*."

❁ Ashley ❁

Two hours later we were in Carolyn's living room, explaining to her dad what had happened. He was clearly upset with his wife for deceiving him.

Mrs. Hamilton kept saying she was just trying to help Larry.

Peggy was white-faced when she arrived and ran to Larry. She finally stepped back and asked, "Why?"

They went into the kitchen to talk, and I knew they had a lot to work through. Mrs. Hamilton had a lot of explaining to do to the police too, and I wondered if she and Peggy would ever be good friends again.

Tim thanked Bryce for following him and keeping him from burning down Larry's house. I think Tim learned that you have to choose your friends carefully.

Carolyn and I had a good talk before we both collapsed from fatigue. I'd like to think she moved a little closer toward God, but only time will tell.

By the end of the day the pastor and others had met with Larry, who agreed to step down from his deacon role and get counseling.

Dustin resisted arrest and actually hit one of the police officers. When Larry let them hear the recording, Dustin was charged with extortion, which means he was trying to blackmail Larry.

That afternoon Mr. Hamilton took Bryce and me to downtown Chicago and the lakeshore. He said we deserved an outing. I don't know how he knew, but he took us to a spot our real dad had taken us when we were little. The water and the skyline were amazing.

Maybe it's true that you can never go home again. Things change a lot. But going home meant solving a couple of mysteries and helping uncover the truth about some friends.

Plus, Mr. Hamilton handed me a check for my work on the commercial.

PART 7

CHAPTER 86

MONDAY

☺ *Bryce* ☺

I snatched a copy of Ashley's commercial and stuffed it into my backpack before we left the Hamiltons'. As soon as we got home, I made a copy and hid it where Ashley will never find it.

That evening I invited everyone to a special event in the living room. When Ashley's face flashed on-screen in that lion outfit, she turned red and threw a shoe at me. Dylan sat enraptured, and Leigh held Ashley so she couldn't turn off the TV.

The outtakes were even funnier. Carolyn tripped over Ashley's tail at one point and fell on a sofa, and you would have thought Dylan was going to bust a gut.

Ashley broke away from Leigh and ejected the DVD, running up-stairs and crowing about having stolen it back from me.

"You think I didn't make a copy?" I said.

"What are you going to do with it?"

"Save it until your wedding," I said. "I've heard you can make some money with stuff like this."

She's still looking all over the house.

About the Authors

Jerry B. Jenkins (jerryjenkins.com) is the writer of the Left Behind series. He owns the Jerry B. Jenkins Christian Writers Guild, an organization dedicated to mentoring aspiring authors. Former vice president for publishing for the Moody Bible Institute of Chicago, he also served many years as editor of *Moody* magazine and is now Moody's writer-at-large.

His writing has appeared in publications as varied as *Reader's Digest*, *Parade*, *Guideposts*, in-flight magazines, and dozens of other periodicals. Jenkins's biographies include books with Billy Graham, Hank Aaron, Bill Gaither, Luis Palau, Walter Payton, Orel Hershiser, and Nolan Ryan, among many others. His books appear regularly on the *New York Times*, *USA Today*, *Wall Street Journal*, and *Publishers Weekly* best-seller lists.

Jerry is also the writer of the nationally syndicated sports story comic strip *Gil Thorp*, distributed to newspapers across the United States by Tribune Media Services.

Jerry and his wife, Dianna, live in Colorado and have three grown sons and three grandchildren.

Chris Fabry is a writer and broadcaster who lives in Colorado. He has written more than 40 books, including collaboration on the Left Behind: The Kids series. You may have heard his voice on Focus on the Family, Moody Broadcasting, or Love Worth Finding. He has also written for Adventures in Odyssey and Radio Theatre.

Chris is a graduate of the W. Page Pitt School of Journalism at Marshall University in Huntington, West Virginia. He and his wife, Andrea, have been married 23 years and have nine children, a bird, two dogs, and one cat.

RED ROCK MYSTERIES

BRYCE AND ASHLEY TIMBERLINE are normal 13-year-old twins, except for one thing—they discover action-packed mystery wherever they go. Wanting to get to the bottom of any mystery, these twins find themselves on a nonstop search for truth.

CP0140